MG Hardie

Presents

Midnight

(Rise of the Black Vampires)

Copyright © 2015 MG Hardie

Midnight and *The Midnight Saga* are trademarks of MG Hardie. Use of these terms is prohibited without permission from MG Hardie.

ALL RIGHTS RESERVED.

This is a work of fiction. Names, characters, businesses, places, events and incidents are either the products of the author's imagination or used in a fictitious manner. Any resemblance to actual persons, living or dead, or actual events is purely coincidental.

Unless authorized in writing by MG Hardie, no portion of this book may be reproduced or used in a manner inconsistent with MG Hardie copyright. This prohibition applies to unauthorized uses quotations, artwork or reproductions in any form, including electronic applications.

The correct citation for this book is *Midnight: Rise of the Black Vampires*. United States, MG Hardie, 2015

1. Vampire. 2. MG Hardie. 3. Title. 4. Fiction. 5. African-American. 6. Contemporary. 7. American Literature. 8. African-American Literature. 9. Romance-Love Story. 10. Religion. 11. Teens. 12. Pop-Culture. 13. Multi-Cultural Discourse. 14. Race-Relations. 15. Relationships.

Contents

Nightmare

"Someday, you will ache like I ache." A brilliant flash, followed by thunder, momentarily drowned out the pounding of my heartbeat. I could feel warmth as his words ripped through my flesh, snapping my head to and fro, driving me deeper into the realm of the dream, the nightmare. Images flowed through my mind's eye like visions from the past. A sexy, muscular man gazed deep into my light brown eyes; his hazel eyes beckoned me to share myself with him.

His gentle kiss, his gaze turned into a vicious glare. His bright eyes cut through the darkness of my bedroom as his hands reached out and seized my throat. His hands squeezed tighter and tighter. The bones in my neck gave way under his testosterone-fueled aggression. The man of my dreams was strangling me.

Chapter One

I saw little difference between my human classmates and myself. I was a little faster, a little stronger, but that seemed pretty normal to me. I was a fifteen year old Black girl and I didn't have my vampire abilities yet. I lived with my father in Beverly Hills, California. I was insulated from the outside world; the breezes, the scents, the sounds.

My father was a hard man with few regrets and I adored him. In less civilized times, he would be in charge of our coven, the alpha vampire. In those days, vampires allowed what was known as The Thirst to rule them. It was simple arrogance that prevented the vampire from living longer than forty years. Vampires had no desire to fit in; they wanted to run shit. Integration for the vampire, for my father, had the same meaning as suppression.

He didn't believe in killing humans, but only because of the war that would follow. I was born deep in vampire country, Savannah, Georgia to be exact. I was born in a simple house that my parents shared. They separated five years prior, before we all moved west to Southern California. I had no reaction to the shake up; I guess I was too young to even notice.

My father and I moved into a plush Beverly Hills condominium to live among the rich and famous. My mother moved to a modest three-room, one-story home in Angel Beach, California. I hadn't spoken to my mother in years because it was agreed that my father would provide all of my vampire necessities. Big cities and vampires didn't mix, so he spent half a decade hovering over me. Of course, when night fell there was always an endless supply of opened blouse women around him.

My father had an acute appreciation of women of all shape and sizes. As long as they weren't all up in my face, his indulgences didn't bother me. My dad and I lived in a world of expensive, luxury cars, precision time pieces, fine dining, and finer clothes.

Both of my parents were telepathic. My mother could communicate with minds; my father could only read them. Telepathy was a female vampire trait. The fact that my dad had any telepathic ability showed that he had taken a different path with his life. From what I had seen, my dad could absorb power from others, but I'm not sure.

My father was slim and muscular, standing about six feet three. He wore vintage hats that seldom left his bald head and he had tremendous vampire swag. He was a man of few words, and since he could read your thoughts, a few words are all he needed. I had never seen this, but the rumor was that my father had telekinesis. Telekinesis is the ability to move objects just by thinking about them. This ability is a power typically reserved for elders. All I really knew was that his irises barely turned yellow when he read my mind.

My father says there were more vampires now than there were before the middle passages.   His father was killed during one of the slave uprisings, which killed dozens of southern plantation owners. He didn't speak about his father and he didn't talk much about his mother. She was from a time when vampires fought, loved, and reveled throughout the night.

Half a century ago when he was very young, a band of humans killed her. For four days, she survived their torture without blood. The elders found her in an old shed, just as her flesh gave way to skeleton. Her body was dismembered and urinated on. My father lived with constant vivid thoughts of this memory. I think that single wrinkle in the middle of his forehead appeared when he had fond thoughts of his mother.

It was important that I stayed safe. My steps were ordered and led to unremarkable days of wearing black that blended into one another. I always felt safe with my father. He always warned me about the dangers of living amongst humans. He told me of the Neo-Nazi's that roamed forests and near beaches, the Klan remnants in Orange County, and the slayers that sought the thrill of killing monsters, even if the monster was only a fifteen year old girl.

My daily blood consumption issue prevented me from attending summer camp like other kids my age. Instead of summer camp, my father and I vacationed in Mecca, The Wailing Wall, Varanasi, and Glastonbury Tor. On those trips, I saw amazing sights, but not as many as I had liked.

I thought the vacations would be adventures, but they always ended up being opportunities for my dad to meet up with old friends, other vampires. My father was always greeted as if he was some type of returning hero.

On those trips, his friends spoke of a time when there were just as many breeds of other animals as there are of dogs or cats... before humans killed them off. I also heard a lot of old vampire spirituals and grumblings of being on the wrong side of heaven. His friends always seemed to have problems with the locals.

When he wasn't tending to me, he drank and partied with his rich and famous friends. They were self-absorbed and less judgmental. He'd tell anyone who'd listen that he was not affected by the poverty, racism, and the learning disability labels that were designed to hold people of color down, saying that he was strong enough to escape them.

We had a two-bedroom condo filled with tufted leather, wooden burnished headboards, vintage film stills, historically significant art, marble floors, vaulted ceilings, rain showers, and an unused pool that we could look through from inside the living room. From our balcony, I peered into heaven with a telescope that dad used to look down on the skyscrapers that populated the Los Angeles city-line. After midnight, he and his friends went out. They returned at all types of hours, but usually before four in the morning. That was how things had been since I was ten.

I had no play dates and few friends. For me, life was pretty simple. It was not like strange things hadn't happened, like my canines descending randomly, or my fingernails growing as soon as they were cut, or having the ability to see in the dark, or dad always winning in blackjack, but the nightmare was something new. And the nightmare was always the same...

Screams ripped through the darkness and my eyes opened. My curls were stuck within the streams of sweat that crossed my forehead. My eyes burned intensely yellow. I looked at the clock, it was exactly midnight. The faint smell of butterscotch floated through the air. My body shook as I scrambled out of bed. My muscles contracted, then slowly released. I tingled all over with electricity. My low cut, cotton, crimson sleep shirt clung to my curves. I was both powerful and weak at the same time.

I lost my balance and leaned against the dresser, my heart rate slowed, I was alone. The only audience for my protruding nipples was the vanity mirror over my dresser. I felt amazing. I reached up and felt blood trickling from my mouth. It was not my blood! I screamed. This was the reoccurring horror that kept me company these last three nights. This is what changed my life.

The repeated clicking of the turn signal pulled me from the isolated corner of my mind. Here I am in the passenger seat of a chrome black-walled Porsche Panamera. It sped along at seventy miles per hour; its soft leather seats swallowed my small body. I hid the bad dream neatly away in the corners of my mind as I eyed my father from the corner of my eye. I knew it was my nightly screams that alerted him. I was in denial all day and was the only thing that I was sure of, was that something had obviously gone wrong.

"You're going to love your new school," the volume of my dad's voice slowly increased. The whole time I was lost in thought, he had been talking. We slowed as the freeway congested with traffic. I could tell that the traffic or the weight of the occasion unnerved him. They, my parents arranged for me to stay with dad until I reached a certain age. As I stared out the window into the deep blackness, I realize that certain age was about three nights earlier.

"Dad, you sound just like a television commercial," I retorted. It was uncomfortable situations like those in which my father sounded cheesy.

"What's wrong with a father wanting his daughter to love her new school?"

"How do you know I am going to love it? I just don't know why I have to move, and to here of all places. I mean, why can't I just stay in Beverly Hills with you, like I've been doing? Why can't I just keep going to the same school I've been going to?"

"Because... it's just that your mother is more..."

"More what?" I interrupted.

"She's more stable than I am. Look, I have my own issues and now you're having these dreams... so your mom and I..."

"You two decided that I should move without even consulting me, without asking for my opinion. Well, it's my life. Isn't it? I'm fifteen years old. I'm practically an adult. I already know what's best for me." I could tell that my father read my thoughts and saw remnants of what I had hid.

"And what, may I ask, is best for you?" he looked over at me through his jet-black sunglasses.

I paused as I looked away from my father to gaze out the window. We passed thousands of lighted billboards and dozens of car dealerships as we speed south on the 405 freeway. My father's mind effortlessly moved the steering wheel, gently coaxing the vehicle from lane to lane. The familiar scent of red grapefruit, saffron, and wood filled the vehicle. We were insulated from the night.

Angel Beach was a large city along the California coastline. Its port was the accompaniment to Los Angeles. By accompaniment, I mean that Angel Beach was one of the busiest port centers in the world. Angel Beach High School had five thousand students and there would be fifteen hundred students in my sophomore class. There were three times as many more humans at the school. The mere thought of it was nauseating. If I was hardly noticed before, I really wouldn't be noticed there.

"I just wish you and Mom had talked to me before making a life altering decision that will ruin my social life," I let that linger for a minute. I didn't remember much about my mother. My father said when they met she made him feel untouchable. He says that she made him want to be a better vampire.

Midnight

"How can living with your mother ruin your social life? You're not being reasonable. There are more things to life, more things to your life, than being social..." he said, looking at his diamond-encrusted watch. It was exactly 11 p.m.

"I had tons of friends in Beverly Hills. So, yeah, I think moving to a new school will ruin my social life. Out here, I will have zero friends, none. All of my friends are in Beverly Hills."

"Now who's exaggerating? You and I both know that you only had a few kids that you even spoke to because you said the kids in Beverly Hills were stuck up."

"You don't need a lot of friends when the ones you have count. They were my friends. It was my decision to talk to them. I had just started to talk to people, now this. It's my life and you are ruining it."

"You'll make new friends, you'll be prom queen before you know it," my father said with a mischievous smile, trying to cheer me up. My father knew I was insecure about my body. "My social life, my friends... everything will be destroyed!" he mockingly said.

"Grown-ups like to say things like that. They always think that they know what's best. I'm the one that's fifteen." I raised my hand, "Count 'em, five, ten, fifteen. I'm fifteen and I know what the hell is best for me!"

"Ambrosia Wharton!" he said, using my full name. He quickly pulled the car over to the freeway's shoulder. "How dare you raise your voice to me!" His fangs bared, and a faint, yellow glow circled his pupils as the sound of his voice rattled the rear view mirror.

"You may be a young woman, but I am still your father. You won't be just another girl by the beach. You must always remember your inherited legacy. You were born where you were born, and you face the future that you face because you are what you are and for no other reason.

"The limits of your ambition are set. You were born into a society which spelled out with brutal clarity, and in as many ways as possible, that you are worthless. You are not expected to aspire, to excel. You are expected to make peace with being invisible. Never forget who you are and what we are. We are the Uhura coven. We are the elite. We are vampire!"

"I know."

"Then, act like it! As a female vampire, it's important for you to be around…"

"Another female vampire," I interrupted my father's lecture. "Yeah, you've told me this a half a dozen times before. I get it; I don't have to like it." I sat uncomfortably silent in my seat. The car's chassis subtlety vibrated from the still running engine. "I'm sorry. I shouldn't have raised my voice."

"Now, that's my little girl," he said with a smile while merging back into traffic.

Traffic cleared as we neared our destination. To change the subject and, perhaps, to end the uncomfortable conversation, he waved his hand, turning the car's entertainment system on.

A techno-hip-hop beat blared from the surround sound system. It was as if the vehicle switched lanes merely from the vibration of the music's bass. He adjusted his glasses as he swayed his head to the musical tune. I put on my oversized shades and slowly nodded my head to the beat as a single tear of depression streaked down my face as we took the off-ramp.

The gritty, rough-and-tumble world of urbanness beckoned to me. Even with the promise of the new, all I could think about was that Angel Beach was a ghetto. We turned down one poorly lit street after another. The lightly pot-holed streets were as deserted as the darkened buildings in which we passed. We made a right, a left, and then a right onto almost blind Myrtle Avenue.

I turned my head and looked at all of the name brand clothing lying neatly on the back seat. All of the major fashion houses were represented in my wardrobe. High fashion and haute couture was mandatory in Beverly Hills. Underneath my glasses, tears began to pool, and formed a small, dark river as black eyeliner ran down my light-brown cheeks. It was 11:30 p.m.

"We're here," he unnecessarily announced as we pulled into the driveway behind a vintage, Knickerbocker-tan, Fleetwood series, V8 Cadillac Eldorado.

The artichoke green, white trimmed three-bedroom house was a few hundred feet away from a corner church and series of low-income apartments. Spray painted graffiti and the word *Killa* were on a nearby red, cement wall. The cool ocean breeze carried the smell of wasted liquor and regrets. I quickly moved the window switch into the upright position as the lingering scent of old marijuana blunts and burnt rubber invaded my nostrils.

"I'm definitely in the hood," I said to no one in particular as I got out of the car. My mother stood on the porch waiting, hurriedly tapping her foot.

"How's my daughter?" my mother's soft voice echoed within my head.

I opened the side car door and gathered my things. "I'd be better if I were back in BH," I muttered.

"Well, you're not in BH, are you? Get your things," the softness of her voice was gone. At the same time, my mother was having a private conversation with her ex-husband as he unloaded my things. My father kept out of the mother-daughter discussion.

"Mom, you know I hate it when do that. It's so vampire," I blurted out. I could tell by the speed my father moved my things into the house that she was telepathically letting him have it.

"Ambrosia... and what's wrong with being vampire?"

"Please, Mom, just call me Amber."

"Well, daughter. I can call you daughter, can't I? All female vampires in our clan have the power to project thought."

"I don't. So what does that say about me?"

"It says that you have a lot to learn."

"Are you going somewhere?"

My mom wore an all-white, flowing robe. She didn't party like dad, but she certainly wasn't a stay at home vampire either. "Female vampires in the coven wear white during the monthly moon blood period, but I am going somewhere."

"Where is my white robe? I'm a female vampire, too," I countered.

"Well, that's one of the reasons... we... decided that you should come live with me. I need to teach you some important things about being a female vampire."

"So you want me to learn to project thoughts too?" I quizzed.

"I... we want you to develop into a mature female vampire. You need a woman's touch, a mother's touch."

"Nobody cares about what I want!"

"What do you want?"

"Nothing..."

"Go to your room..."

I entered my room, slammed the door, and plopped down on the new teakwood bed, thinking of the future. I got up and

Midnight

filled my closet with the clothes as my eyes filled with tears. Sadness erupted from me like lava from a volcano.

In the condo, my bedroom was full of cute, little stuffed animals. A drawer sat against the wall and my desk set was in the corner. My social world in Beverly Hills, the world that mattered most to me, was coming to an end. I couldn't believe that I was forced to give up that life for the hood. I was hit by a wave of feelings and all I wanted to do was lie on the floor and cry, but something held me back. That something was the noise of my parents arguing in the living room.

"Well," my father said matter-of-factly, "she's your daughter."

"When she behaves like this she's my daughter, and when she gets A's in school, she's your daughter, right?"

"Well..."

"She's *our* daughter. Your job of protecting her is now over. Would you like some tea?"

"After all of these years, you are still patronizing me. I know what you're really thinking."

"Well," she said while pouring a small cup of Camille tea. "I am glad you told me about the dream, but let me tell you what I think. I think you party too much. I think you drink too much.

You are hardly around enough to give her what she'll need to handle what comes with these puberty dreams. I think this self-indulgent, uppity lifestyle is a bad influence on our daughter. Do I need to mention your temper and your distrust of...?"

This argument made it seem like their separation was only moments ago instead of five years. It was one of those arguments that made them relive the bad times, but, somehow, even their most painful memories were beautiful to me.

I organized my room, unaware of the nature of my parents' conversations due to the periods of noted silence from the living room.

"There is no need for us to argue, it's simply in her best interest to live with you for a while," my father said, not wanting to rehash any previously held animosities between them.

"What do you mean for a while?" My mother raised her hands toward the roof to center herself and her thoughts.

"I mean, this is not a permanent move," he explained.

"What our daughter doesn't need is to be moved back and forth between schools. It's not a stable upbringing for a growing young woman. You thinking that it's okay is part of the problem!"

"Let's not argue. Let's come together for our daughter's sake."

"Let's commune... Amber!"

Communing was the way vampires shared their love for one another. Through their souls become one—one soul, one heart, one mind, and one blood. Three or more vampires could commune, and in that way they could feed off of one another. It was a séance that brought the essence of the vampire's soul into connection with other vampires within the Uhura coven. I walked out of my room to join my parents in the living room. We formed a circle and held hands, ready to commune.

We transfixed our gaze into the empty space between us as our souls co-joined like Siamese twins attached at birth. When our vampire powers triggered, our light brown eyes transformed in color—becoming bright yellow, well, my eyes were little more than yellow sparks. We joined with each other and with others in the Uhura clan as images flashed of what had brought us to that point.

Voices whispered the name of the elders and the name of the coven. The Uhura coven was an ancient coven of Black vampires. The legend of our coven extended beyond ancient Chaldea in Mesopotamia, near the Tigris and Euphrates rivers, and beyond the land of the Chaldeans, which was the original home of Abraham. The vampire was the offspring of Lilith, the first woman and first wife to Adam.

Lilith was beautiful and strong willed. She was Adam's equal and refused to submit to him. That refusal caused her to be forced out of the Garden of Eden. After leaving the garden, she hid near the Red Sea. Upset and still in love with Adam, she allowed herself to be ravaged by cast down angels. Those that were cast down fathered thousands of her children.

God sent Archangels to her with orders for her to return to Eden, but she remained defiant and rebellious. Her refusal was the original sin and it sealed her punishment. Archangels commanding twelve legions, descended upon the Red Sea, killing thousands of her offspring. Lilith and the fallen angels tried to fight them off, but there were too many. After all of her children were dead, God cursed Lilith and limited her bearing of children.

God cast down The Fallen One into the darkness, only to land in Lilith's bed. Once there, the dragon grew to love the very thing that caused the war in heaven in the first place, a human. Their passions gave rise to a seed, a seed that for all time would become known as vampire.

Because of God's curse, the goal of each coven was survival, and that was why each vampire's birth was a celebration. Naturally, each of the covens had a difference of opinion on what was best for them to survive. Occasionally, the clans ran into disagreements with each other, but the elders respected one another and disputes typically ended quickly. The mating of Lilith and Asmodai, Satan's third in command, produced the Vampirin that formed the Sammael coven.

The Sammael coven thrived from hatred. It was named for the hellish underworld where vampire spirits once frolicked around burning fire and brimstone. Members of the Sammael coven's eyes became sky-blue when their powers were activated.

The Sammael brood was respected, but factions within it were rabid and quite blood thirsty. Some of them were disrespectful vamps fueled by bigotry, sadism, and violence. They blamed God for the torment and eventual destruction of our foremother. It was an offense they simply could not, and would not forgive. In general, vampire beings hated the seed of Adam and Eve. They exist with an unsettled pass, for them their only true enemy was humankind.

I have never felt like this before, we communed and a newfound peace found my mind. The spirits of the coven assured me that it was in my best interest to live with my mother because being a female; I was going to need all the help I could get to develop and mature.

As soon as the communing was over, my father looked at us, said "umoja," and then he finished unloading the last of my belongings. He looked down at his watch, the time was exactly midnight. He donned his crimson outlined, double breasted, black trench coat, quickly hopped back into his car, and speed away, back toward Beverly Hills. He didn't say goodbye because he didn't need to. In the deepest sense, the vampires of the coven were always together in spirit.

Midnight

"Baby girl, you have to make your own decisions, your own choices. You have to live with the consequences of your choices. I will be here to help you learn and grow as a healthy vampire being," my mother told me. "Come here; let me get a good look at you."

"Yes, ma'am." I silently stood next to my mother in the living room.

"My, you've grown. You're taller than me now."

"Maybe a little."

"I am really glad that you are here. It wasn't easy to get you into Angel Beach High. Vampires have no room for sorrow. You have to make your own way. Let me make it a little easier for you," she said as she gathered her beautifying tools.

My mother sat on the couch, I sat on the floor between her legs, and she went to work on my hair.

"Some rhythms never come clean. Life is tragic simply because the earth turns," she said as she brushed my hair. "The sun rises and sets and one day, for each of us, the sun will go down for the last time. Perhaps, our trouble is that we will sacrifice all of the beauty in our lives, will imprison ourselves in totems, taboos, crosses, blood sacrifices, steeples, mosques, races, armies, flags, nations, in order to deny the fact that death is the only fact we really have.

"For the vampire, we ought to earn death by confronting it with passion. Life is that small beacon in that terrifying loneliness that the vampire must embrace. The vampire is nothing without love."

And, like that, she was finished with my hair. The speed which she did it was only limited by the tools she used. By the time she finished telling me what she expected from me, my hair was done. It was crafted to medium long lengths throughout, just long enough to hide my dimple, but still allowed for movement of my ends.

"I totally love it!" I said excitedly, as I looked at myself in the living room mirror. "I have to wrap this."

I really did love it. It was soft and it was cute. It enhanced my natural highlights. I'd been doing my hair since I was ten, but my mother had a talent for it. She put my ponytail skills to shame. I thanked my mother with a hug and walked into my bedroom. Mom left me alone to finish unpacking. I looked at my hair in the mirror, and thought, *it's nice to be allowed to be myself.*

I guess I understood my parents' reason for the move. Maybe they were right, maybe tomorrow would be a new day, a new moon, and I'll be a new student. Angel Beach High school's year had already begun and the students already knew each other. I am going to so hate being the new kid, the new kid from Beverly Hills. No one wanted to be the outcast.

With a million people living in the city, I may not be the only vampire in school. The Spanish-speaking Qayin coven was in East Los Angeles. Quick-tempered Gabriel de la Cruz was well known and the head of the coven. The Qayin coven came from the demon Kukulkan, who Lilith also mated with as she fled God's wrath. Qayin's were known for their artistry. They trafficked drugs into the United States; it was their little way of getting back at humans. They were very territorial.

There are a few covens around and then there were the Albinos. The Albinos made their presence felt at various high schools in Southern California; nobody crossed the clique. They were descendants of the Nordic god Odin, and their lore was passed through Zeus. The Albino clique was worldwide, but a smaller sub group resided in Orange County, California.

Midnight

There were thirteen members of the clique and they all had
blond hair and pale skin. The females were disgusting and
gangly. The males were at least six feet tall, they were strictly
pack vamps. If you saw one, the other dozen were hidden.
They were the vampires that humans usually read and heard
about. They are poor excuses for vampire. The albinos live in
a frat house they called Valhalla.

They didn't respect anyone or anything. The albinos were
far less civilized than the garden variety vampire. They liked
their blood with a little flesh on it. They would drink the blood
of anything, and I mean *anything*. They had no problem taking
down a deer, dog, possum, or a squirrel, for that matter.

Their skin was devoid of natural sun block, so they were
even more sensitive to the sun's rays. They could become
badly burned, blistered, or even blinded within minutes of
extreme exposure to the sun. Because of their lack of melanin,
they were not as fast, strong, or as beautiful as Black
vampires. Their powers are weak, but they were still
dangerous and blood thirsty. The mongrels feasted on flesh
and when they did, their irises turned red.

My parents were not fond of the albinos, who weren't really
albinos, they are just white vampires. The albinos viewed low
hanging, human fruit and suicidals as blood donors. Albinos
viewed taking these humans off the street as a public service;
they took care of those that evolution missed. In Southern
California, attacks on humans had become more frequent and
the Albinos were quite messy.

Albinos were obsessed with mating strictly with their own
family members to keep their blood free from the *Dirty
Bloods.* Historically, these inbred vampires were allies with
the Sammael coven. They were lawless, unruly, and
unpredictable. Their skin tone allows them to fit into

dominate first world cultures. There were more Albinos because their skin tone had caused them less persecution throughout the centuries, but the numbers of vampires of color were growing. Sadly, bits and pieces about these subjects was all I learned from eavesdropping on conversations.

As I unpacked the cardigan sweaters and A-line dresses, my mind was filled with hundreds of what-ifs. I had a lot of nice things. I was not really the superficial type who placed too much emphasis on fancy clothes and possessions. I was not looking for attention, especially now. I had clothes in every color, but I often wore the color black because it suited my mood. Besides, since I was a vampire, I figured I may as well dress for the role. When I wore black, I felt more mysterious.

I looked at myself in the floor length mirror. I was not thin or thick. I didn't have the shapeliest body, but my clothes fit. I see at myself as a canvas whether I am wearing a plunging white halter or gold wing tipped heels. I continued to fill my drawers with cheekies and boy shorts.

My closet was lined with bodysuits that I would never dare put on. My wardrobe was simple, yet cute. It may seem a little androgynous, but it was fashion flexible. You wouldn't find any bold bust lines amongst the saddle shoes and riding boots. Unlike most teens, I don't bury myself with too many colors.

Even my cotton cami and pajama shorts were cute. More often than not, I slept in a comfy sleep shirt. I put my two-piece, silk Batwoman pajamas on the bed. Even in my sleep, I had to stay classy. My ensembles kept me balanced. They say the darker the vampire, the stronger they are, so my brown skin was a source of pride for me.

Midnight

My dad had wonderfully dark brown skin. My mom's chestnut skin was darker than mine. My skin was chocolate like a perfectly blended coffee, my lips were thick, and my body was athletic. In three hours of unpacking I had pondered my entire life. The move had turned a long day into a longer night. I went into the bathroom; I would baptize myself into the new life.

I turned on the shower and briefly looked at my reflection in the mirror. I looked at my almost shoulder length hair, my brown skin, and my brown eyes. I saw the reflection of a five feet six, brown, monotone being with a few moles here and there, but nothing special. My breasts, well, let's say they were still loading.

There was no getting around the fact that where I should have curves, I had edges. Earlier when my dad was here, I saw him getting an eyeful of my mother. He says mom is a brick-house. She was a beautiful vampire, and I was unremarkable and thin.

I stepped gingerly into the shower and let the water rinse over my smooth skin. It felt good, warm. Soon, I was lost in the shower. So many thoughts ran through my mind. I told myself that things would be okay. I slowly got out and dried myself off with a thick, red towel.

Weakened by the shower, I leaned back against the wall. I looked again at myself in the bathroom mirror. I saw something I didn't see before. Now, I saw strength and determination. In a few hours, it would be the dawn of a new day. It was about four o'clock. I put on my silk pajamas and crawled into bed. I fluffed my pillows as I cuddled up into a ball.

I hoped to sleep well my first night in Angel Beach. The tears that I expected to soak my pillows never materialized.

Hopefully, my dreams were pleasant ones. I closed my eyes and sleep came quickly.

Familiar screams caused me to open my eyes. I have a confession to make…

My name is Ambrosia Wharton. My friends call me Amber. I'm an African American
                Vampire and I've just killed again.

Chapter Two

I hadn't killed anyone, it was all a dream. The orange curtains in my room allowed the low morning sunlight to nearly blind me. I needed to get up, but my queen sized bed was comfortable. My mother had my bedroom filled with hideous abstract art, which was the first thing I was going to change. Against the wall was a large oak drawer. My computer set on a vintage wood desk in the corner. A small, white block couch filled with colored pillows was on the other side of the room.

I pushed my closet open, pondering what to wear for my first day of school. I was glad that my parents didn't buy me school clothes; they bought me life clothes that I wore to school. I imaged what the city would offer me as I slipped in and out of various clothing selections. I stumbled into the kitchen, half awake.

"Daughter, how did you sleep?" my mother cheerfully asked.

"I slept well," was all I managed to say. That was a complete lie because my vivid thoughts were still with me, but I also knew that she couldn't read my thoughts without me knowing. The breakfast she made looked great, dad never cooked a meal for me. I sat down at the table and prepared to eat.

"It's your first day at your new school, are you ready?"

"I guess that I have to be ready, don't I?" I countered.

"That's good to hear, now eat your breakfast." She gestured toward the eggs, sausage, and pancakes. There was an ice cold glass of chicken blood near my plate. To avoid drinking human blood, we drink animal blood.

Most covens drank animal blood. Contrary to popular belief, vampires needed to eat. We also needed an ample supply of blood. Most used the blood of chickens, cows, sheep, and deer. The easiest blood to get was chicken blood, so that is a staple in vampire households. The more active a vampire was the more blood they needed.

In a dark wood paneled pantry, there were three small refrigerators; these are used to store blood. One was for chicken blood, the second was for blood of animals that were animals with hooves, such as deer, which were closet to human blood, and the third was locked. That one was for human blood.

Human blood is the most powerful of all blood. Human blood that is not connected to the life force loses some of its power. It must be cooled quickly to prevent it from spoiling. Drinking warm human blood that was connected to its life force produced an addictive high. Without blood, a vampire wouldn't last long in direct sunlight. Vampires were strong, but lose their abilities when the sun rose. Blood countered that.

I covered the pancakes with maple syrup and bit into the sausage. The warm juice slid down my mouth. It was good. I didn't know she could cook like that. As I ate my breakfast, I reached over and grabbed the glass. With one quick gulp, I drank it down. I licked my lips, tasty. It was the perfect way to wash down my delicious breakfast.

I looked admiringly at my newly painted red fingernails. My almond shaped fingernails looked and felt like glass. They were sharp, hard, and they grew really fast. Instead of hiding them, I kept them painted with multiple coats of polish.

Bright sunshine was all I could see from the front window of our house. It was time to begin my life at a new school. In some ways, I was being born again. The horrible thoughts were forgotten.

The interior of the house was different from how I remembered it from my single visit five years prior. Mom had completely redecorated the house with African art. Tribal masks hung in the living room. Some of the masks had slits under the almond shaped eyes and long faces. The masks represented the spirit of our ancestors. A guardian mask was above the front door. A large picture of Martin Luther King Jr. hung prominently in the dining room. The walls were white and all of the picture frames were black wood.

My mother was a do-it-yourself kind of person, which was another thing my dad didn't like about her. She painted the walls, tiled the kitchen, planted her own food, and she decorated the living room center-pieced with a multi-sectional couch that was white and blood red. There was a plethora of elegant mirrors that hung throughout the house.

She owned a salon that was called Venus. It was a large, white and black painted salon that was on the corner of Pacifica and Waterfront Street. The salon's front window proudly displayed a large, electric, cursive red V inside of a red circle. After they separated, she bought this house and opened a hair and nail salon. It was one of the best hair and nail salons in the city. It was so popular that the clientele nicknamed it 'The Showroom'.

My mother's room was in the front of the house. It was a nice sized room with antique furniture and a vintage, queen sized mahogany bed. As I walked through her room, I was surprised to see a wedding photo on the dresser. It had been five years since they separated and I still found myself searching for evidence that they would get back together.

They were married twenty years ago on a Savannah beach. They had a night wedding with a scenic view of the shore and neighboring islands. Five years after they were married, I came along. I knew that they were bonded, but I think the only way they could truly love me was if they got back together.

Angel Beach had several man-made islands and schools that only existed because whites fled the oncoming brown to the city. Half a century ago when Blacks started to move into Angel Beach, whites moved to the outskirts to shield their children from the onslaught of brown skin. They created outlying communities, neighborhoods, and hid schools. Naples was the most popular of Angel Beach's islands. It was small, but there were many lavish mansions that were not far from expensive shopping centers and yachts that gently bopped in the bay.

On my mother's dresser, there were pictures of me when I was little. There were washed-out photos of me riding a bike and throwing a ball. There was even a dreary photo of me taking my first step. In that photo, I was wearing a bright pink, polka dot dress. I bet she thinks these photos are cute, I think they are embarrassing. I didn't even like pink. Apparently, my parents liked to dress me in bright colors.

I walk through my mom's house, our house, toward the door. My parents were as different as night and day, but it would make me feel good inside to know that she still has love for him. I wanted to know if she kept her love for him in a photograph. I put on my reddish brown drop earrings; they dangled a few inches above my clavicle. They were the only pair of earrings I had. I looked at the person staring back at me in the mirror one last time and sighed deeply. I turned to one side and posed. I was glad I was not paper thin.

It was time. I decided to walk to school. And just like that, I started a series of firsts. Mom didn't bat an eye when I told her I was walking by myself, as if she expected it. I reached into my pocket and pulled out my newly given house key. The sun was in rare form, the heat from it felt heavy.

Hummingbirds darted in and out of the bushes, and the sparrows rustling in the willow tree in front of our house were having a heated discussion. I closed the front door and locked it behind me. As soon as I closed the door to my house, I heard the loud thump of drums and the horns of the school band. When the drums stopped, I heard the shouts of the cheer squad.

There were a few other students just off my block walking to school. They laughed with each other and listened to music. They didn't see me. I was invisible, even in the light of day. I was unseen. Damn it, I was already a spook. Kids walked by me as if I was standing still. It had only been one block, but I felt like turning back. Maybe this was a mistake. The new girl was a creature not to be worshipped, but shunned.

I strolled down New York Avenue with my black boots gilding across the sidewalk. Not paying attention caused me to trip over my own awkwardness. I sat in the grass trying to center myself before I made another attempt to get to school. As I got up, I wished my father or mother were there to hold my hand, or that they at least had the good sense to think about what they were doing when I was conceived.

They had created a being that, at the age of fifteen, would be so invisible, that the possibility of ever being happy was a fantasy. I was fairly sure that when I was conceived they both thought they were goddamn geniuses. A sane person would not chose this exile, where were my transgressions... My moment of feeling sorry for myself was interrupted by the loud chirp from everyone's cell phone, an *Amber Alert*.

The loud intrusion on everyone's electronic device indicated that a little white girl was missing. That sound meant that for a brief moment the channels that were usually dominated by images of Black bodies dancing, singing, debating, performing, or dying, would now fill timelines and newsfeeds by whiteness.

Angel Beach High School was three blocks from my house. The neighborhood looked different from how I remembered it, but five years was a long time. Gone were the randomly abandoned shopping carts and the impossible-to-escape barred windows.

There were more lightly colored houses than apartments, Guadalupe palm trees and simple gardens dotted my frame of view. I stumbled again, but this time I tripped over a raised piece of uneven sidewalk while I watched the fox squirrels dance on the trunks of large oleander trees.

Last night it looked like a ghost town, but there was life here, people lived here, a lot of people. Some people were on their way to work or walking dogs. The neighborhood looked middle class, but it was still that place where when one person was shot, all the people around that person were forced to retaliate. The violence spreads from one group to another, from one community to another like an infectious disease going from body to body, it was still that place.

By the time I reached the end of the block, my body ached. I didn't sleep well, I had tripped three times in two blocks and my breakfast blood was still powering me up. The sights and sounds on the way to school were overwhelming; it was a good thing that I always had my earphone and shades nearby. I was never without an assortment of clips, bands, colorful wraps, and matching shades of lip highlighter. Today, I was not wearing lipstick.

It was too hot to dress in all black, so something different was in order. I sauntered down the street in a yellow Aztec print shirt showing as prominently as to contrast with my stitch, electric tomato skinny jeans and super skinny yellow belt. I'll have to use make-up to age me, but not now and perfume dulled our senses.

I made it to Chain Break, a bike and coffee shop a block away from Angle Beach High. I ordered a house coffee, then sat and sipped the house blend as I watched the streets slowly congest with hundreds of vehicles that dropped off students. There were teenagers everywhere, students from all walks of life. I began the final leg of my journey. Unlike many kids, I waited for the green light to cross the street to enter the large school parking lot.

In Beverly Hills, the students represented the upper class. Here, the school parking lot looked like a cross between a bustling open air market and a pop video. There was no shame here. The Angel Beach parking lot was filled with fancy cars, old school hoopties, a few scooters, and pimped-out whips. Half of the kids wore jeans so low that they threatened to reveal where the Lord split them. A Hip-Hop song from a Ford Impala with a chrome grill shook the ground just as I reached the parking lot.

I slowly made my way through the parking lot as the hoodied hordes moved in and out. Students wore skateboard shoes, but had no skateboard. Other students had on tight skirts, shirts, and skin tight jeans that helped display subtle midriffs. A couple of girls displayed not so subtle midriffs to highlight belly button piercings and tattoos that led down to the nether regions. Some students wore beanies, designer glasses, and gold chains.

School security patrolled the roof with their eyes focused on the activities; they were armed. A group of kids were doing the latest dances as the music blared in one section of the parking lot. In that far section of the parking lot, they rolled deep and had their pants cuffed. A few of them were doing a gangsta dance and waving hands with their fingers twisted. Of course, that action drew peculiar looks from students passing by. I could hear security on the radio running toward that area.

"This definitely isn't Beverly Hills," I quietly said to myself as I entered through the school's main gate.

"Did you just say Beverly Hills? Are you from Beverly Hills?" a voice shot out from behind.

The voice caused me to stop. I cringed and turned around to see a cute Asian guy. It was too hot to wear a long, black trench coat, but there he was wearing it as he leaned on the wall. He looked like the coolest thing in the school. He wore eyeliner and an earring dangled from both ears. His hair was slicked back and he looked like a Goth, metro-sexual television show winner without socks.

"Yeah, just transferred in from Beverly Hills High," I sluggishly responded. He was the first person I spoke to at my new school and it wasn't so hard.

"So, you were in the 90210 with the rich kids?" he asked.

"Not all of them are rich. I just went to school there, it's no big deal," I explained. "Besides, I'm here now."

"My name is Jonathan Diep, you can call me Jon. My friends call me JD. You are Ambrosia Wharton, right?"

Midnight

"Ummm... call me Amber. Wait, how did you know my name?"

"I know everything about everyone."

I became fully embarrassed by the unwanted attention. I looked down at my schedule of classes. More than ever, I just wanted to make it to my first period class, Mr. Emmett Taylor's Chemistry class.

"Jonathan... ummm, JD, do you know how to get to Mr. Emmet Taylor's Chemistry class?"

"Of course, that's in Building A, just follow me."

The noise of students going this way and that sounded like the hum of a noisy washer. We briskly walked past the newly cut hedges and across the plush greenery of the large quad toward Building A. It seemed as if a thousand eyes were on me and I was wilting from the heat and the uninvited stares. The banality of my sophomore year was now punctuated by the stares of newness.

"It's a bit intimidating, but you'll get used to it," said an animated Jonathan. "There are various groups here. You've got the Whites, Blacks, Hispanics, Asians, those are the large groups. You also have sub groups of Mexicans, Puerto Ricans, Columbians, Vietnamese, Cambodians, Koreans, Africans, and Pacific Islanders. On your left, you have the rich kids, the smart kids, the popular girls and guys. On your right are the ultra religious, the big talkers, and the druggies. In the middle, you have the activist, the rebels and jocks, the gangstas, and the girls that love them."

"What about that large group?

"Oh, that's the group of people who don't know what they are. And, you see them over there? That's the militants and idealist section. Mixed into all of those groups are the quiet ones, sluts, hos, and your garden variety trouble makers, but I don't judge. Most kids come to school to get some form of education, but there are some kids who only go to school to jack kids, they're jackers."

"Jackers…"

"Meaning they'll jack you for your shit! Anything they can't steal, they'll break. If nothing else, you have to watch out for them."

The buildings and gates that surrounded the quad closed off the school from the outside world. I wasn't used to seeing metal detectors at the doors and armed officers in the hallways. It seemed like an hour had passed before we reached the Chemistry class and just in time for the bell to ring.

The class was a large room of black-topped, smart lab tables with a stack of chemistry books on each table. Two students sat at each table. Mr. Emmett Taylor, the Chemistry teacher, wore a button-down Polo shirt with a pocket protector filled with ink pens, stood in front of the class. He was balding and had a large belly. There was a name plate on his desk that read in an overstated way *Mr. Taylor-Chemistry Instructor*. I entered the class and stood nervously near the door. The teacher's old, brown eyes looked in my direction.

Turning to me, he said, "You must be our new transfer, Ambrosia Wharton."

"Just Amber."

"Ok, just Amber. We are well into the semester, so you'll have to get caught up. Let's find you a seat."

My brown eyes slowly scanned the room for a comforting face. I felt twenty-five sets of eyes shift toward me, waiting on any movement from me. Those five seconds before I moved to find a seat seemed like an eternity. *Yes, find the outcast a seat, shall we?*

Midnight

"We'll have you sit next to Adrian Reznor. He will help you get caught up," said Mr. Taylor as he pointed to the left side of the room.

I looked around the room expecting to see some goon or a stereotypical nerd who needed a better relationship with lotion. When I first laid eyes on Adrian, I no longer felt like crawling into a hole and dying. He was a handsome guy, African American, and muscular with perfect lips. His muscle definition was highlighted by the fit of his neatly pressed white Polo shirt. His hair was styled into two neat cornrows.

I'm definitely going to sit next to him. As I took my seat, my nostrils caught the scent of something, his blood. My mouth watered as I sat next to him.

"Hi. I'm Amber," I whispered to the stranger.

"I'm Adrian, nice to meet you," he whispered back with penetrating, light hazel eyes. He was handsome and polite—winning.

The school was getting better by the minute. Mr. Taylor talked about the basics of chemistry while I thought about my lab partner that was inches from my hip. For some reason, I couldn't get rid of his scent. I could tell what body wash and deodorant he used that morning. It all made me squirm a little in my seat.

As I sat in that seat, a clawing began inside of me. I flipped through the textbook and didn't notice the other students. I didn't know him, but I felt as though I did. I took notes as the lecture continued. I briefly glanced over and noticed that Adrian took detailed notes. I wrote *Matter and Energy, and the interactions between them.*

As fitting as the chemical reaction lecture was, my mind remained on the boy I sat next to. The boy I'd just met. I found most human males unappealing, but not him. I couldn't explain it, but my senses were going wild. He was about six foot three and athletic. He wore new *Jordan's* and form fitted blue jeans. An elegantly carved red acacia cross dangled from his neck.

The lecture finally ended. He started to get up, but then he adjusted his shoestring necklace and turned toward me.

"It's hard being the new girl, huh?" he said, already knowing the answer.

"Yeah, I just transferred from Beverly Hills High."

"Beverly Hills. That sounds nice," he offered.

"It was a nice school, but I'm glad to be a student here. New beginnings and all..." I tried to sound down-to-earth, but I was sure I sounded like I was trying too hard.

"Well, I've got to go. I've got basketball practice next period." Adrian got up from his seat. My mouth hung open as I slowly watched all six foot three of him rise.

"So, you are on the basketball team?" I asked the obvious question.

"Yes, I'm the shooting guard," he explained.

"What a coincidence. I plan to try out for the girls' basketball team," I said, reaching to find something, anything.

"That's cool. I hope you make the team," he said as he put his handheld computer into his backpack.

"See you later."

"Sure," he softly said as he left the classroom.

He didn't know it, but I felt as if I just spent an entire lifetime with him. What was going on with me? I looked at my class schedule: Chemistry, Spanish, Physical Education, Lunch, Geometry, and English. So, my next class was Spanish in building 515B. I pulled out a map of the school and headed down the long hallway.

Midnight

"Hey Amber, how is your first day going?" a familiar voice asked from behind me in the crowded hall.

"So far, so good," I offered. It was Jonathan. The Vietnamese-American kid I met when I first entered the school.

"What class do you have next?"

"I've got Spanish with Ms. Sanchez."

"I have that class too." Jonathan excitedly said. "Follow me." He led me down the crowded hallway.

Jonathan leaned toward me as if he was going to whisper a secret in my ear. "Remember when I told you that I know everything there is to know about everyone in the school?" I nodded my head, affirming that I did remember. "I wasn't just bragging, it's true," Jonathan said with a hearty smile. "I go to all the parties. I attend all of the sporting events, well, all the cool ones anyway. I am a member of all the student clubs. I'm even a member of the student council, I'm the treasurer!" Jonathan bragged out loud.

"JD, what do you know about a guy named Adrian Reznor? I just met him in Chemistry class."

"Adrian? Oh, he's strange."

"Strange how?"

"He's a Christian, a real one," Jonathan started. "I don't see how a person could be that devoted to a religion. It's kind of creepy don't you think? I am not even devoted to these ankle boots I have on right now. Do you think I should change them?"

"JD!"

"Okay, the dude's got game. He's the only sophomore on the varsity basketball team..."

"That's impressive," I added.

"He's an only child from a very conservative, evangelical Christian family. His father is a pastor and he always has a bible handy. I don't think I have ever seen his father smile. His mother is a housewife and she makes the best peach cobbler in town. I can't wait for sophomore carnival. She makes these graham cracker pies with a little cinnamon on top…"

"Ahem…" I said, rolling my eyes.

"Right… The Renzors are very serious about their beliefs and his education. He is a top students and he doesn't really go to parties. They live in Belmont Heights, which is not too far from the ocean. It's actually a nice neighborhood, but too quiet if you ask me," Jonathan concluded.

I was impressed and disturbed that Jonathan knew that much information about a person. Adrian was a Christian and Christians didn't believe in vampires. I thanked Jonathan for the information and continued walking to Spanish class in silent reflection. The teacher was Ms. Sanchez, a short, full-figured woman with dark brown hair. As I walked in the door, she greeted me.

"Are you the new student, Ambrosia Wharton?"

"Please… call me Amber."

Once more, the outcast.

"Ok, Amber, you can take this seat in the front of the class. Now, before we begin class, I want you to introduce yourself to the class in Spanish," Ms. Sanchez said with a suppressed smile.

This is embarrassing… This is embarrassing… This is embarrassing…

I looked into the sea of unknown faces. I know I am a new student, but I didn't want to be treated like a new student.

Midnight

The bell rang, and I rose in front to the entire Spanish class to introduce myself.

"Hola. Yo soy Amber. Es un verdadero placer estar aqui con ustedes," I said, which meant, 'Hello, I'm Amber. It's a pleasure to be here with you.' I quickly took a seat. Ms. Sanchez nodded her head and let out a low, "Hmmmm." I figured that a little showing off might keep her from trying to make any further examples of me.

The Spanish lecture seemed to take hours, mostly because Ms. Sanchez insisted on conducting the entire class in Spanish. Even students who could barely speak English slowly muttered and prattled through it. Good thing I had Spanish at my old school so my Spanish was pretty good.

My next class was gym. The main gymnasium was next to the outdoor basketball courts on the far side of the school. I got dressed in the girls' locker room. We were forced to wear green shorts and yellow t-shirts, which weren't very fashionable. About thirty students sat on the bleachers of the basketball gym. Mr. Ferguson, the Physical Education teacher, stood in front of us as his two assistants quickly rolled large basketball racks across the court.

"Today, we will be doing basketball drills," he began. "We are going to go over the fundamentals of basketball. New girl, you don't have to be as good as a professional basketball player, just try your best," Mr. Ferguson said without even looking in my direction. Within minutes, we were two organized rows passing the ball back and forth to each other. Each time Mr. Ferguson blew his whistle, we changed direction.

Defensive slides, hands up, hands down, and bounce passes were standard drills. The exercises were no problem for me because I always played basketball with my dad. If he weren't vampire, he could be a professional basketball player. I had been forbidden from playing on any team, out of fear that I might lose control. My dad knew himself, but he was more afraid of what I might do.

Next we did layup drills. Starting from the free throw line, we were instructed to bounce the ball three times and then lay the ball into the basket. There were some students whose heads were ahead of their skills. They were the ones who had watched too much television and tried spins, tricks, and cartwheels on the court. They were also the ones who usually ended up hurt or sitting next to Mr. Ferguson, and no one wanted to sit next to him.

Then we practiced dribbling the ball up and down the basketball court, right hand, and then left hand. The assistants broke the promising students up into smaller groups for other drills. In groups of two, we sprinted from one end of the court to the other while bouncing the ball. The class was co-ed, so boys and girls did drills together. Then we did the three-man weave, but when we ran suicides, that when students started grumbling. Only a handful of us completed that drill, a few students kept right on running out of the gym door.

Some girls from the varsity basketball team were in the class. I was one of three picked to run a five-on-five game by the assistants. Adrian entered the gym and watched from the stands. I made a crisp pass and set a good screen. Then I eagerly harassed a girl named Monica. I stole the ball from her and went coast to coast for a layup. The girl seemed to take my defense of her personally, which she should have.

That girl was Monica Jones, a junior, and the starting guard on the varsity team. The year before she came off the bench Angel Beach didn't win the title, but she had an all-city season. Even though she didn't start, she led the team in assists and steals, and right now her sights were set on me. She called for the ball and I got into my stance. She crossed the ball over in front of me and I quickly launched myself at her. Another steal, she fell trying to protect the ball. I raced forty-two feet for another layup. I jogged back on defense; the gym was silent.

It was the first time Mr. Ferguson looked up from his clipboard. The big clock in the center of the gym stopped ticking. All you could hear was the sound of sneakers on the hardwood court as I deflected another one of her passes. Somehow, within that fifty-five minute class, an epic rivalry that seemed forged over centuries had developed.

Monica was grabbed my shorts and put an elbow into my side as I pivoted. She was pretty strong. Out of the corner of my eye, I saw more students entering the gym. I heard the whispers, felt their eyes turning to us. I couldn't back down. First, I stepped left, she reached, I crossed over, and she was off balance. I dribbled into the lane and dropped a behind the back bounce pass to our center for an easy layup. A collective sound of oohs and ahhhs came from the students.

I heard some in the crowd say, "Who is that?"
The whistle blew it was time for everyone to hit the showers. Monica pushed the basketball into my stomach and glared at me as she walked off the court.

"You're Amber, right?" said a smiling Mr. Ferguson, as I walked passed him toward the locker room. He motioned for me to come over to talk with him, so I did. "You play well," he said to me in an understated still gritting his teeth way.

"Thanks."

"Just in from Beverly Hills High, right? Who taught you to play basketball like that?" he said, looking through paperwork.

"I only play with my father," I explained.

"I am the coach for the girls' varsity basketball team and I'd like to have you on our team. We could use someone like you."

I promised him that I'd talk to my mother about the offer. Of course, I wanted to be on the team. With Physical Education class over, it was lunch time. I quickly walked home for lunch thinking of the fresh supply of blood waiting for me. I was so thirsty.

I walked out the school and darted pass the small coffee shop on the corner. Soon, I was at the front door of our house. I took out my keys and opened the front door. My mother was at her salon, so I was alone in the house. I went into the panty, took out a large pitcher of chicken blood, and poured it into a cup.

I sipped blood and thought about my first day at school, a day full of double takes. There were a lot of awesome people at the school. I thought about Coach Ferguson and the boy I met in Chemistry class. I raised the cup in my right hand with a sly smile on my face. I said aloud, "It's great to be a vampire."

I downed a glass and a half of blood before returning to school.

Chapter Three

I saw the half-eaten possums, heard the music, felt the heat of a bonfire, someone was carrying me—just another dream. I was awake and there was nothing like the smell of freshly cut grass mixed with gunpowder in the morning. And, just like that, my second week at Angle Beach High began.

Roberta Flack softly floated through the house. As always, I looked at myself in the full-length mirror and asked, "*Who am I?*" before I left the house. I teased my eyelashes and was off to school. I kept it simple with mostly black attire.

My hair was pulled back into a ponytail. Strangely, there wasn't a cloud in the sky and the sun was puttin' in work. The heat from the sun randomly blocked the cool ocean breeze. The best thing about my second week was that I knew exactly where my classes were. Well, that and I only tripped twice today.

Each day, faces became more familiar and, of course, Jon was always there. Today, he was decked out in gold *Vans* shoes, purple skinny jeans with an oversized white Lakers jersey. His fingernails were painted royal purple and gold. One thing about him was he knew how to dress.

"Ready for week two?" he asked as we strolled down the center quad area.

"So far, so good," I replied as we walked.

In Angel Beach High, there was just about every nationality present, a lot like the real world, except everyone, for the most part, got along. Most students came from a working class background. That diversity allowed students to interact with people they would never have otherwise.

At my old school, most of the students were extravagantly wealthy. Beverly Hills High's parking lots were always filled with expensive luxury vehicles. Many students had multimillion-dollar trust funds, so they never needed to fill out a job application, or work a day in their lives.

They had wealthy parents, and those parents made certain the school had the latest technology available. The Beverly Hills High's media center had the latest, rarest books, and top notch computers. The parents also made sure influential guest speakers were on hand to lecture the student body.

Wealth has its disadvantages. Rich people had problems, they divorced and they die all the time. Children with money had intact families, but most were not raised by their parents. They were raised by maids and nannies. Their parents didn't sit down to talk with them; they bought gifts and pretended that everything was okay.

There were affluent parents who picked up their children that attended Angel Beach High, too, but they did not linger on this side of town. The police handed out a lot of speeding tickets after school. The hood and Beverly Hills weren't so different, the villains just looked different. In the affluent areas, gangs still marked their territory one with legislation, the other with spray paint. The glaring difference from both places was that the wealthy made sure their children knew their rights.

I knew if I was going to get along in the new school, I had to stop thinking about my old school. In order for my new school to accept me, I had to accept it. Schools were only as good as the students that attended them, and Angel Beach High was as good as any other.

Midnight

I was happily on my way to first period. I was excited about the class for two reasons, because I enjoyed the subject, and because I got to start the day off watching Adrian's chest go up and down. Chemistry was a fundamental component of every being. Perhaps, there was something going on with me and Adrian, maybe it was just me. I didn't know what it was, but every time I sat next to him, my mouth slowly began to water.

As Jonathan detailed the latest he said, she said gossip, my thoughts drifted towards Adrian's shoulders. He was on the basketball team and my mom allowed me to be on the girl's varsity squad, how could things get any better? I love the velocities, the angles and the mathematics of basketball, but how much of myself do I show...

Last week, I used most of my daylight power trying to impress some boy. That power had to be replenished. When I drank chicken blood I can physically compete with humans. Vampires were weaker than humans, which was why we must have blood.

I made it to class just before the bell rang. Jon whispered, "See ya," and slowly shuffled off to his next class. As I walked into Chemistry class, there was a caramelized blood aroma, and there was Adrian. He wore a white cotton t-shirt layered underneath a turquoise v-neck sweater and blue cargo pants. I took my seat next to him and my heart began to pound, no, raced.

I felt an uncomfortable aggression. My seat next to him seemed more like a pit I had fallen into. A pit I couldn't seem to get out of, that I didn't want to get out of. I thought I had a handle on everything, but I no longer knew where I ended and he began. I felt as if I was being pulled to him. The new feelings left me uncomfortable.

"Today, we are going to discuss basic atomic structure. By the end of this lecture, you will have a fundamental knowledge of protons, neutrons, and electrons," was how Mr. Emmett Taylor began his lecture.

I liked Chemistry. I liked the idea that matter could be broken down to its various parts. That meant that nothing was exactly what it appeared. Everything had a fundamental essence at its core. I took comfort in the thought that everything was made up of atoms.

I liked the idea that everyone and everything in the universe was connected. On the surface, we all appeared different. Some people were tall or short, some brown or white, and a few vampire and more human. At our fundamental core, we were all made up of the same atoms and shared the same space. For me, Chemistry was not a class about atoms and molecules; it was a course about us, all of us. Near the end of Mr. Taylor's lecture, Adrian and I had a quiet conversation.

"I watched you in P.E. last week."

"Really?"

"I was pretty surprised, you being the new girl and all. There aren't many girls at this school that can play like you do."

"Maybe I am just full of surprises. Do you want to see me dunk?" I asked, hoping he'd say yes.

"Hey, I said that you can play, let's not get carried away." He chuckled.

"Whatever, it got me on the team. After school, my first practice is in the main gym. You should stop by and I'll give you a few pointers," I told him in reserved way. I don't want to seem overeager.

"I'll stop by just to see you, uummm dunk..." He smiled.

Midnight

"Aren't you the only sophomore on the varsity team?" I asked curiously.

"Yes, that makes two of us. I would like to play professional basketball."

"That's cool. Who are you favorite players?

"I love Jordan. I like Kobe, LeBron, and Iverson. I try to learn something from each player. I patterned my game after Oscar Robertson," he said, demonstrating his basketball intelligence.

"I like Candice Parker and Serena Williams...I also play tennis," I said, not wanting the conversation to end as I look slowly around the class.

"Wow, is there any sport you don't do?"

"I like all sports, but I would love to represent the United States in the Olympics," I said, but that was a convenient lie.

"You have to set big goals in life. My parents always encourage me to follow my heart, especially my dad," he whispered.

"Do you like rap music?"

"I love it. You have to be aware of how the masses are living."

"I like it too," I said, realizing that we were still in Chemistry class. We really should have been focused taking notes, but weren't.

Suddenly, he turned to me. "After your practice, do you want to go get a latte or something?"

I couldn't believe it. He was asking me to go somewhere with him. It was not a date, definitely not a date. I mean, it was a latte.

"Sure," I said.

"Ok, I'll be there after my CSU meeting."

"What is CSU?"

"It's the Christian Student Union. I'm the president,"
I glanced down and focused on the carved red acacia cross that hung around his neck. I felt weakened. Some Christians believed that vampires were demons. I looked away from the cross and sighed. I hoped he was different.

"That's great," I said in order to mask my doubts. I looked up and the lecture was over.

"See you later."

"Fo sho."

I left class and headed down the hall toward Spanish class. I ran into Jon again, he was not alone. Three students flanked him all wearing various coats, even though it was quite sunny.

"Amber, let me introduce you some of my friends," Jon began. He pointed to a tall, well-proportioned girl with a mocha complexion.

"This is Tiffany Davis."

"It's nice to meet you," I said while shaking her hand. "I like your earrings."

"Thank you. A family of third generation African-American jewelers made them.

"They are beautiful."

"I'll make sure to give you the website."

She was a pretty girl, but not that pretty. She wore eyeliner, black lipstick, and green, yellow and red African onyx earrings to go along with her black pea coat and a very forgiving a-line skirt.

Jon gestured to a Hispanic kid. "This is Carlos Gomez." As I shook his hand, I noticed that he had tattoos on the back of both hands. *Live Free* was written in cursive on back of his right hand, on back of his other hand it read *Or Die*. He had three earrings in both ears and wore heavy eyeliner. He had on an open jean jacket, some cute jeans, and a print top that read *Stop Looking!*

Jon gestured to the other Black girl. "And, last but not least, Holly Thomas." She was shorter than Tiffany. She was pretty with light brown eyes and full lips. She had a bistre skin tone to her. Her eyebrows were finely curved and plucked to perfection. She was short and curvy, but not fat. Well, she was not fat to me, she was bottom heavy. Underneath her denim coat, she had on a cute, floral print, heavy metal shirt.

"So, you are into rock music?" I said to Holly.

"I'm into rock, heavy metal, and everything in between," she answered.

Jon turned to me and said, "Since you are new here, I thought you would like to hang out with some of my friends. I thought we would have lunch together in the cafeteria."

"I would like to but..." I hesitated and then said, "Sure, I'll be a little late, but I'll be there."

I'd be late because I needed to go home at lunchtime to drink a glass of blood. It was a ritual that I had to maintain to keep me strong throughout the day. I should be able to walk home, power up with my hemoglobin energy drink, and get back in time to meet them in the cafeteria. The week before I spent a lot time being alone and eating lunch alone, and I didn't like that much.

After scheduling a lunch meeting, JD and I hurried to Spanish class. I entered with him by my side. Slowly, I took my seat near the front of the class. With our portable computers enabled, I told mine to turn to page seventy eight. We were going to do Spanish verb conjugation. We were learning the verbs Ser and Estar, which both meant "to be" in Spanish.

After Spanish class, I headed straight for the gym. We ran laps. I didn't know anyone who liked running laps, even I didn't like them. The track extended near the football field to the far side of the school. In the locker room I put on my running shoes and the standard P.E. uniform. I pulled my hair back and was ready to go. We took our places on the field. Most students were in various stages of shape and most were not good.

"I am going to use the whole semester to get each and every one of you to get into shape. Today, you'll be running for exactly thirty minutes around the track," Mr. Ferguson bellowed. He must have been in the military or something because he was a real task master. Mr. Ferguson is also the head of the athletic department, so all complaints go to him.

He loudly blew the whistle and we started jogging around the track.

"Hot as it is, and he got us runnin' in circles and shit!" someone complained.

I jogged as I was told. I felt the cool wind softly blowing on my body. I could smell the very human scents of the other runners on the breeze. It was almost overwhelming. Female scents I could deal with, but the scent of human males was almost repulsive. I told my mother about the new sensations and she said that I was becoming more aware of my vampireness. Drifting through the air, I could smell sweat and blood, and, once again, I was very thirsty.

After the run, I quickly changed clothing and headed home for lunch. I took out my key, popped open the door, and walked to the pantry. I was salivating. Being around so many humans running and sweating had helped me work up an appetite of blood.

I opened the refrigerator and poured a tall glass of chicken blood. In a few minutes, I drank two glasses and started to feel my energy returning. I exhaled and began the walk back to school for my lunch meeting. I entered the school at the side gate, made a right, and headed toward the school cafeteria.

The cafeteria was a rectangular building with several large windows that opened outward. There was a buffet style set up where students waited in line and choose the items they wanted to eat and drink. It wasn't hard to find JD and his three, black-clad friends sitting in a far corner. Talk about sticking out. They were almost finished eating when I made it over to their table and sat down.

"Hey, Amber, are you going to eat?" JD asked, seeing me without any food.

"I already ate," I said, picking up a cracker from Carlos' plate.

"So, how do you like the school so far? Is it as good as the BH?" asked Tiffany.

"It's diverse, that's for sure. It is starting to feel like home," I offered.

"Don't you miss the rich kids and your champagne problems?" she countered, looking at my clothing.

"Not really. For me, it's what's inside a person that counts," I said as I watched Tiffany's throat expand as she took a bite of chicken fried steak. I watched Holly slowly wash down her food with milk. They couldn't tell, but they all had crumbs on their faces. They seemed so satisfied when they ate.

I liked talking to Tiffany. Her questions told me that she was actually paying attention, or maybe it was her dark style that made me feel that we were kindred spirits.

"There are a lot of different people here," said Carlos

"Carlos, tell Amber about your tattoos," JD said as he drank soda and stuffed his mouth with potato chips, half of which fell on the table.

"These two tattoos are important to me," he began. "My right hand says live free and my left says or die. Together, it's the sentence, 'Live free or die.' Everything is a choice. Life is a choice, so is death. You sitting here with us is a choice. There are choices we make every day, every moment, and every second of our lives. If we don't choose to live free, then we have chosen to die.

"This sentence is special to me because I am also different. I just turned fifteen, but I have known for years that I'm homosexual. This summer, I came out to my parents, and they have accepted me just the way I am. They told me that it doesn't matter if I'm gay, straight, or whatever, they love me and that I'll always be their son. I got these tats after I came out... I'm sorry..." he said as tears from around the corners of his eyes. The revelation must have caused him and his family some pain, it was still raw

"Carlos, I'm glad that you felt comfortable enough to share your feelings with me. Everyone should feel comfortable in their skin. Most people have problems accepting others because they deep down inside haven't accepted themselves. Never apologize for who you are," I said to Carlos. There was a noticeable silence at the table.

"Sooooo, I hear that you are interested in Adrian," Holly Thomas blurted out.

"Jonathan!" I scolded.

"Girl, don't worry, it's cool. He's a nice guy," Holly said.

"Sorry," Jon said. "I couldn't resist the urge to spread a little gossip about the new girl."

We all laughed as we sat at the end of the long table in the cafeteria in the corner. Carlos told me about the future events at Angel Beach. Of particular interest to me were the end of the year barbecue and the year end dance.

Midnight

"Yo, Jonathan are you from Vietnam?" someone across the cafeteria yelled.

"I'm from Westminster," was JD's smiling response.

Just as the bell sounded to end lunch, JD pushed a button on his wearable arm piece, a song played and he and his friends got up and performed a thirty-five second hip-hop dance.

The dance seemed well rehearsed, but they were totally free styling. The performance was filled with isolations and anticipations of each other's moves. They had real physical intelligence; I was in awe of them. They didn't need to be given a stage, the world was one.

At these lunch meetings, we talked about teachers, school, and our classes. When we were dressed in black, we look like a Goth clique. We only wore all black for the looks we got. When other kids stared at our version of teenage rebellion, I would smack my lips and subtly reminded them that it was how awesome looked from the outside.

Chapter Four

The more time I spent with my new friends, the more at home I felt. It didn't take long for us to turn each other's looks and phrases into inside jokes. Every day I sat in the school cafeteria with my new friends, talking, joking or vice texting. My social world was forming into something stable, something meaningful.

Once in a while, Adrian stopped by my practices and sometimes we walked to get a latte or something. When he and I were together outside of school, there was always talk of keeping it real, but I was the only one not doing that.

My second week in Angel Beach, the popular girl crew tried to bully me. Ignoring them didn't work and telling the teachers didn't work. The girls walked the halls like they owned them and everyone in them.

These girls went out of their way to be unpleasant to people. They messed with people who would remember the particular unpleasantness decade later, but the popular girls would forget their actions five minutes later. That was when Jonathan didn't really even know me, but he was quick to step in to defend the new girl.

He eased up when I said, "I got this." Nowadays, you have to get up pretty early in the morning to best me. I went from zero to bitch real quick. It was funny as hell when I told them off.

"They think they are bosses, but them broads is special, Amb." Tiffany added and like that, I got a nickname and a reputation. Monica, our point guard, was in that popular group.

MG Hardie

My dad says, in life, someone is always going to talk shit. How you handle it is what matters. Kids have a name for people like that— haters. Haters were always quiet when they were by themselves. Monica's best friend is Irene Baxter and she's a hater. She's at every practice over sharing and demanding that people called her *I-Rene.* Unfortunately for her, I didn't respond well to demands, so she could just stay salty.

The fact that I was on the varsity squad rubbed some people the wrong way, especially Monica. Even I was confused when they bumped and pushed me in practice. They tried to make broken plays seem like my fault. On the court, I was efficient, I didn't waste moves. Every time I got in a tournament game I turned it into a track meet. I drove the lane in traffic. I took charges. I kept going when my opponent stopped. Good performances in those holiday tournaments made my teammates trust me. No turnovers helped with that.

Now that Monica and I were on the same team, her tone had definitely changed. Well, her tone towards me changed. To the popular girls, the only thing that mattered was appearances. They cavalierly tossed around gaudy phones that flipped into tablets and necklaces that monitored biorhythms. They viewed three hundred dollar clutches and two hundred dollar heels as cheap. They looked down on anyone who purchased off-the-rack.

I couldn't remember exactly when I stopped wearing designer fashions, but I did. You won't find me carrying overpriced bags emblazoned with an emblem so large it could be said that it was out of place. I no longer wore clothes that showed that I overspent or that I was for all intents and purposes an unpaid model for their products.

Midnight

Day after day of watching these fashion scenarios play out, I just realized that teenagers, single handedly supported the fashion industry. I do have to give it to Monica though, she worked hard on the court and made military jackets and studded combat boots look sexy.

Coach Ferg was firm, but he was fair. He was a good motivator. Basketball to me was just a game, but to some students basketball was a way of life, a way out. For them, basketball was hope. The hood provided just a s many young bodies willing to put on a nation's uniform as it did those willing to run and jump for hope.

Angel Beach High had sent more people to the NFL than any other high school in the country. It was named athletic school of the century and was yearly ranked as one of the best high school athletic programs in the nation. Students from all over the nation wanted to attend to Angel Beach High for a chance at athletic stardom. The school's football games were televised on cable.

Angel Beach was not just about football and basketball; they were also highly ranked in volleyball, track, swimming, and even badminton. The school's music program had won nine Grammys. The walls in the main school hall were lined with trophies and awards. Most students never stopped to truly embrace the rich history and tradition that was Angel Beach High's.

You wouldn't know it from looking at the area, but families relocated just so their children could attend the school. Angel Beach High was the destination for many students, and other schools were a distant second choice. *Home of Champions and Scholars,* was on the banner that hung in every hallway, the school lived up to that motto.

Angel Beach was a blue ribbon school with twelve learning academies, two were magnet programs; one was called the Additional Curricular Experience or ACE. ACE was a take no prisoner program that brought in and challenged the best and brightest students from around the country. It had the most sophisticated honors and advanced placement classes in the nation.

Everyone had to be in a program. Adrian was in the ACE program, and I was in the Technological, Entertainment, Academic, Media program, or TEAM for short. I was starting to like being a Guardian that was our mascot. Since I transferred after the school year began, I had to wait until the next year to get into ACE, but the program I was in suited me.

I am a movie buff. I watched all kinds of films, new ones, old ones, documentaries, dramas, and comedies. Somehow, watching a movie with commercial interruptions sanitized the movie and dirtied up the commercial. I dislike dance films, reboots and films where the actor causes a huge explosion and never looks back at it. Those films insult intelligence.

For me to truly love a film it had to be more than just a film, it had to move me. Movies were simple escapes. On my blog, I critiqued these theatrical intersections of sex and violence. My most popular blogs were *Why the term 'All men are created equal' leaves no room for women?* and *What do bikinis have to do with car shows?*

I was lukewarm to the idea of being on the basketball team. My mother really pushed the idea. She probably thought I would just sit on the bench and cheer my teammates on. I felt at home on the court. Once the season started we practiced three times a week with a game at the end of each week

In practice, I usually let Monica get the better of me. She was the starting guard and I was the first one off the bench.

Midnight

We were most effective when we were in the game together. She was a junior and had only one more year to get good college scholarships; I wasn't going to take that away from her. Playing basketball used a lot of my energy so I had to increase my daily intake of blood. I was now drinking a glass of deer blood a day.

Every night I put on a dark hoodie, fingerless cowhide gloves and lightly scaled the nearest fire escape. I easily climbed up structures and scampered across rooftops. Shunning gravity's traditional effects, I leaped from car tops to awnings with ease. I perched on low hanging tress, leaped from window ledges and balconies, and landed without a thud.

Aside from wandering the city at night, my friends and I had developed a routine. Sometimes they stopped by to watch me practice and after practice, posted up at Chain Break, hung out near the beach, or played video games at someone's house, unless Adrian had a game, of course. For his games, I always tried to get a good view.

Adrian's eyes shifted from brown to green, they were multicolored with a green ring around the edges. His eyes were like summertime. If you asked me, I thought things were going quite well. It might sound melodramatic, but I literally felt that my life changed the moment I looked into his eyes and smelled his sweet blood.

I acted a little weird when I heard conversations and sounds that others didn't, or when I saw things no one else saw. I didn't mind being the weird girl that brought a lunch on our adventures. It was actually kind of refreshing that people thought I was the square in the group. I was far from the perfect vampire. I got caught up as well.

Of course we could all get together and watch movie debuts at home, but we all rather go to the theater. Outside, we were out, we could be wild. When the friends got together outside of school, sometimes, we acted ignorant. Once we were all thrown out of a movie theater for being too loud. I still didn't know why I led that cheer, but the movie was boring and we were teens. That day Tiff said, "Would you like Adrian if he wasn't on the basketball team?"

"Of course, I would," I quickly responded.

"But, being on the team is a plus, right?"

"It's definitely a plus," I smiled.

All the girls in the crew talked about sex, but I was sure that none of them were panties-on-the-side-of-the-bed with another person sexually active. Besides, even three days after a person has showered I could smell the unique scent that a used condom left on the body. The people who talked the most about sex were the ones usually not doing it. I didn't think you could resolve every conflict with sex, but it was done, so maybe you could?

When the teenage groups get together, there are healthy barrages of, "My nig," "First of all," "Bruh", "Wus good", "Bitch, please" and other assorted phrases tossed around. You'd be surprised how long a person can do Deez Nut jokes. We were bit more respectful when it was just one group. My father told me long ago that intelligent people spoke slang on their own time.

Thankfully, and because of the blood in my diet, I didn't have to worry about pimples, zits, or rapid weight gains or losses. And that's a good thing because those superficial conditions seemed to bring humans an inordinate amount of worries, no matter how small the pimple or weight change.

Midnight

If a girl is paying attention she notices how people react to her based on what she is wearing. People react differently to if you have on jeans than they do when you have on a skirt. They approach you differently if your hair is on tilt. When people approach you, you can feel the animal instinct coming from them. It's the animal inside of us all. Some people ignore it, some use behaviors to their advantage and some don't know what to do with it and it scares them.

Then there are the people who don't want to be approached, talked to or even looked at, so they change how they dress. They take care to wear muted colors, put on baggy tops and pants and they don't use bright lipstick. From where I sit every night I watch everyone and everyone is pretending, no one is really themselves, no one is comfortable. And all the effort they take to hide only serves to make them more uncomfortable.

The thing is that they aren't really paying attention to each other, but there is always someone who thinks that look is about them. They think you asked them out because you saw their legs. They don't raise their hand in class because they don't want the eyes on them. They don't want their thoughts to be discovered. They are afraid they'll be wrong, they are afraid you'll see the real them. Humans are so busy hiding their flaws they've made themselves paranoid.

I could always feel my canine teeth moving. A dozen years ago was the first time I can remember my fangs coming out, it was painful. They just started growing. I didn't know what to do. I was crying and that was the day I was I was told what I was. That was the day I became the scariest thing out. They no longer hurt when they elongate, I am just working on controlling when they extend when they don't. What is a vampire without... control.

MG Hardie

It is liberating to be able to say anything I choose to say, or to wear any color I choose to wear, being afraid is a choice. Humans fear for nothing, or should I say the wrong thing. All of my female friends have been told not to walk alone or go out late at night. Those warnings didn't apply to me. For me everything that's wrong, feels so right, so I wish a nigga would.

I didn't say a lot, but I had new friends that I liked and they liked me. In my little group, we talked about relationships. I have to speak in general terms because I didn't know what a real relationship was and also because I didn't want people all up in my business—girls could be messy when it came to rumors and gossip. JD was another story.

I smiled when Tiffany's thick, curly hair peeked out from underneath her brown Negro League baseball cap. She says Black people shouldn't pass each other without acknowledgement, so she always has respect head nod handy. You won't catch her with a Lincoln Theodore Monroe Andrew Perry smile.

She admired how I dressed. She didn't need to front about not having money around me. She'd tell anyone who'd listen "I'm not trying to be understood, I'm trying to understand," but her pride wouldn't allow her mouth to form the sentence, *Can I borrow those shoes?* Even though the shoes looked good on me, I managed to find ways of getting her into them because that was what sistas did.

Tiffany always talked about black power or how Africa is the motherland, but she could save the stoic act for someone else all I saw was hurt. Just don't let her get started on how Black people forgot that white people stole us or that Black people built the pyramids and sailed the seas long before the white man came out of caves. When she was on one of her rants, it's best to just to leave her alone.

Tiffany's mother was a strong disciplinarian. Her mother was real nice to me, but she didn't tolerate children talking back. Tiffany's leg welts and cigarette burns were evidence of her mother's intolerance. Tiffany preferred to be someplace other than home. If there was any type of gathering, you could find her there.

I would be the first one to put on workout clothes and head to the park or the beach, and Tiffany wasn't far behind. Whether we were out, or just trying on clothes, she was my set it off girl. She had to get out of the house and I enjoyed being out of the house. I used to be sad when I see her running and splashing in the ocean water. Instead of hating on her from the sideline, I let her do her. I was not missing out on the ocean. It looked clean, but it was not. Though, I did occasionally dip my toes in the water.

Tiffany is going through a lot; she wasn't concerned with having a relationship. The first time we had a conversation about race, we were sitting on the lighthouse benches. I out looked across the ocean and soaked it all in, and said, "It's a trip how Black people pre-date everything."

Tiffany looked up, took a sip of her kiwi infused water and said, "Look at how far we have come. Not long ago, Black kids were amazed that another Black person had a color TV or a microwave. Black people opened the eyes of the world to our strengths and talents. Blacks protested, marched, and voted because they wanted what they thought was the impossible."

"Until a thing is done, it will always seem impossible."

"Yes, but those wants were misplaced?"

"Misplaced how?"

"I mean, marching without a power base, and no plan ain't nothin' but a parade. We are beyond wanting to drink from an outlawed water fountain, beyond not being able to sit anywhere we wanted on a bus, but we ain't beyond being shot by the police on general principle. Some of us have gone straight to wanting to live in good areas, driving a fancy car, or going to a good school.

"Once they didn't need us to build this country, they incarcerated us and used us economically. They contained and influenced Black people and we settled for being equal to whites. We never get tired of wearing these cultural costumes, it's sad. You'd think that after all the things brown folks have gone through. The one thing we should be paying is attention."

"I know, right? It is like progress stalled somewhere, ain't nobody post-black. We settled for education over freedom. How can you want better when you don't know what better is?"

"Girl, we something else. We can't just be calm. We are too conscious. We can't be respectable with people who aren't respectable."

"I refuse to be stuck in a world where the dark heroine is everything but dark."

"Lions, Tigers, Bears, Elephants, Sharks, animals just attack 'em. Tornadoes, hurricanes, earthquakes is just killin' you, even the sun don't like you... They anti-natural and you gon' listen to them about how things should be...naw... naw!

"They fed us what equality was and we ate that shit up. If we didn't come together only after a tragedy, it would be harder to manipulate us. It's so bad now that black folks are in control of the destruction of black folks."

Midnight

The rest of the day we didn't speak much. She didn't open up to everyone the way she did with me. She was one of the more conscious people that I knew, her age notwithstanding. Tiffany's militancy is a healthy display of her anger, it's healthy, it's the match, you can't just chant your way to first class citizenship.

Since I moved to Angel Beach, I had to make some adjustments. For example, I now enjoyed the simple things and I had to. The only extras my mom had was extra flat irons, extra curling irons, and extra chores. There were no trips abroad and no dry cleaning. I had to wash my clothes, paint my nails, and do my hair.

Mom managed to take a day or two off to hang out with me. She took the day off to take us girls to the snow covered mountains. I skied, mom disappeared and everyone else sled. Tiffany had never touched snow before; her whole face lit up when she did. We had more adventures without the extras.

Mom played D'Angelo and Lauryn Hill on the way up the mountain and telepathically told me tales about when she was a young vampire. Like the time she arrived in Kinshasa just in time to see Ali knock out Foreman, how she came to be an extra in the film *Purple Rain*, and how fond she was of lighters during the Los Angeles uprising. My giggling had Tiffany and Holly messaging me nonstop.

I believe that she was in the stands when Dominique whipped her Perfect ten, but I find it hard to believe that she was Janet Jackson's back-up dancer, sat on the greens when Tiger Woods won his first Masters or that she was at the Neighborhood Ball when Barack and Michelle danced on his first presidential inauguration night. She also claimed to be there when the internet muted parental authority... like I'll just believe anything.

Holly was the queen of shopping. Often we would go to four stores to get a shirt, and she made that fun. She had very good taste and she was the only one in our group that worked, even if it was part-time at a little downtown boutique. I was pretty sure she was well over her spending limit. She could do something about her weight instead of maxing out her credit card trying to be accepted. The girl can sing though, she had mutant lungs.

She says she's too cute to hike, jog, or do just about anything that required being physical. When we were in the mountains, she keeps saying, "Y'all go ahead, I'm cool right here." Her parents ignore her; of course, they fawn over her thinner, prettier, younger sister.

Holly is currently crushing on a guy named IsAnthony Scott, or IS as they call him. They say he's a thug. I mean, fighting, jacking, slanging, you name, they say he does it. His muscles looked like he spent half his life in the penitentiary and he was tatted up like it, too. He and his home boys didn't discriminate; they were always surrounded by an assortment of girls.

In his familiar growly tone he regales us with tales of lawlessness and loving the coco. He had a philosophy of trying to keep his necessary dirt confined to white people. The word is that he's was incorrigible, but don't use that word when you talked to him. He took words that he didn't know the meaning of as disrespect.

He was known around school for giving people the big F and the small U. "I'm ah buck dat foo," "I 'on't play no games wit deez niggas". "Get tha hole puncher", "Don't test ma hood", and "Don't hustle backwards," were his signature lines.

Midnight

I had English class with him and believe me when I say the slang was strong with that one. I was often amazed that I could understand him. When he's in class, he's actually a good student. He stepped over just enough lines to get kicked out of class, but not out of school. He was the kind of kid teachers offered other teachers two-for-one student exchanges for.

Wearing a suede leather beanie and plain black shades, he leaned against the wall just outside of class long after the bell had rung.

"Mr. Scott, the bell rang," said a passing administrator.

"I heard it," was his response.

From what I'd heard, he didn't return phone calls, texts, or greetings, but Holly said, "He's a keeper." He'd been tazed and tear-gassed; he was about that life. He'd be cuter if he didn't always go so hard in the paint. I don't think he even notices Holly. She always tries to be around him, hanging on his every word.

You know, it's amazing how the wrong guy seemed to know all the right things to say. Last Friday, Holly convinced us to hang out with IS and his North Angel Beach homies near the shore. An hour later, sirens were blaring and he and his partners ran off...while repeating the murmuring cadence, "IS, IsAnthony Scott, mess around wit me and yo gon' get shot!"

A smile danced on Holly's face as she looked me dead in the eyes and said "Girl, he's just misunderstood."

"By who, the police?" I said incredulously.

"You respect the OGs because you'll be older longer than you'll be younger, and then what?", he once said to me. "Look how all these youngsters say they want to be rich; they just never think they'll do it by selling dope. If it weren't for Black people, White folks would be killing each other. They can get away with killing us."

He said things in this country were this way not because of race, but because of money. The racial aspect is collateral damage. He was nowhere near dumb. He taught me what dry-snitching and self-snitching was.

The first time I picked up my vampire power was a vision fragment from IsAnthony. One day school security had him hemmed up against the wall. In his mind, I saw him with his grandmother. He nursed her. He picked up her medication from the pharmacy. Her social security check didn't cover all of her medical expenses, so he paid the bills.

I saw him in those fleeting moments' in-between bouts of punching the jaw of another teen when he briefly wondered if what he was doing was wrong. I saw him make certain his cousin stayed out of gangs by making sure he got to football practice on time. Most of the time, he did what he wanted, but some of the things he did because had to. People like him were reminders that just because someone maybe a proud hoodlum, it didn't automatically mean they weren't valuable.

As school security yelled at him and pushed his face against the locker, I wondered was it his fault that he was born into a world that he could never be prepared for? Was it his fault that he was taught how to hide from the police long before he could spell? Should he not be angry that he was treated as a problem long before he was treated as a person? Was it his fault that he wasn't noticed until he took something that wasn't his? Should he not be angry that he had to be conscious of his hand speed when reaching for gum? Was it his fault that those around him were more human than they were hero? The answers were no, no, I don't know, maybe, no, and the fault was ours.

Midnight

People wanted to be like IS. Every day I saw the worry on the faces of students, but his life was beyond getting a "D" on a midterm paper or staying out all night at the beach and having the marine police take you home just so your parents notice you. When he wasn't around, students imitated his attitude, his walk, or the way he spoke. They imitated him right up until the police showed up. He lived like he had nothing to lose, because he had nothing to lose. They don't make niggas like him anymore.

Growing up, he didn't do any more dirt than other bad actors. His skin tone just made the spotlight brighter on him. He didn't create the society, he adapted to it. You had to respect him, if you didn't; he had a way of putting people in their place.

One Saturday, we were all out and Matt Livingston, quarterback of our football team and Leanina's boyfriend, took issue with his presence with our group. Matt's issue probably had more to do with tight shirt IS had on more than anything else. That shirt made him look ripped when he wasn't even trying and he wasn't trying.

Matt went in on him with, "You know all I hear from you is nonsense and poorly used curse words. I don't hear intellectual thoughts, no music, no poetry... you're just a common hood."

"Just a common hood," was IS' tilted head response. I held my breath because IsAnthony doesn't let people run off at the mouth.

"Yeah... a thug," Matt continued.

"Hey, boys, calm down now. We are all friends here," Tiffany chimed in.

"Friends, and a dumbass." They laughed.

"Can you read, playa? I'm being serious. Who is the best poet you've heard?" said Matt.

"I'm the dumbass, huh?" IS said. "At any given time, there are fifteen to twenty motherfuckers rapping about having more money than the next guy, all competing to be *The Next* for the young niggas like you to cheer while going out to copy the latest dance and fashion hoping, just hoping they could be like them while they smile smugly and intellectualize about what they would do differently and how stupid those in the spotlights all are.

"It is people like you who take all routes to consume lies and to speculate on shit they have absolutely no interest in, but never lift a finger for hours on end to help a kid that's struggling with their math homework. Those same children smile while attending mandatory classes to be ignored and have nothing, but genetically modified cereal treats hurled at them to satisfy their nutritional needs.

"Why would anyone read if reading produced a big two scoops of raisins, young front, old back, peach fuzz havin', larvae face, arrogant fuck like you? Now, to answer your question, it isn't often, but every now and then I am the best poet I've ever heard."

The whole time he calmly spoke, Leanina was aroused. I have to admit that even my eyeteeth moved. That was the last day I saw her with Matt, you should have seen her eyes glaze over. Thug, hood, or just human, the guy tried to change his life the best way he knew how, the only way he knew how. And, there I was wandering around the city, afraid of being found out, afraid to even whisper on the lightest of breezes that I was vampire. Everyone I knew had no control over the circumstances of their birth—he, she, and they hadn't given up, and I admired them.

Midnight

Of all of my friends, Carlos was the only one that was paranoid. He thought everyone was talking about him. It had to be hard waking up every day knowing that the people you loved and cared about wanted you to be anything but gay. It was Halloween and Carlos went all out. If it weren't for his flair for glittery Goth nail polish, I wouldn't have known he was the big red Z Tetris piece. I, of course, dressed up as the *Invisible Woman*.

My actions may be free of moral convention, but I see everything. Sometimes there are things you don't want to see at night. Everyone has an agenda, look at the pretending that saving boys isn't saving girls. It's all pretty absurd. It's easy to be culturally Black around other Black people. It's easier to be a vampire at Halloween.

Halloween gave everyone an excuse to dress up like a sexy tiger this, a sexy nurse that, and a whole lot of other things that you knew don't go together. Some students had on gorilla, goblin, and creatures of the night costumes. As part of my routine, I always found an excuse to pretend to be human; I guess it was okay for humans to find an excuse to pretend to be a vampire. I thought I deserved an academy award for my portrayal of a human.

Most vampires accept our place among humans, though they have hunted and killed us, still we smiled in their faces and acted like it was all good. Maybe it was the vampires that were fakes. From what I had seen, tolerance didn't freely exist within the human mind. I hold back because I couldn't ever imagine coming out.

Chapter Five

In class after class I sat being pulled between two worlds;
one human, the other vampire. My family and I were
vampires; all my friends were humans. I hadn't forgotten my
vampire history. I hadn't forgotten black history, but new
feelings and sensations drove me. I was a very good student,
but now I can seem to focus on my class work.

I thought I was doing a pretty good job of separating the
biracialness. The ebb and flow of the struggle pushed me in
one direction and tugged me in another. The walls that
protected me began to cave in on themselves. In addition to
my school work I had to drown out pounding heartbeats and
random conversations. There was some kind of theater was
playing itself out. There were characters, plots, subplots, and
roles to be played, and I was but one. In my role, I had
thoughts of biting anyone, everyone.

So far, my nights had been pretty tame, I explored but I
hadn't traveled far from home, but tonight was different. I
found life about four miles from my house. I was there when it
happened. The neighbors looked out of their windows as a
young man who was visiting his newborn son was gunned
down in a hail of bullets. He awkwardly fell to the ground as
his life force slowly made its way out of him. He lay in the
middle of the street in the warm sweet and sour chicken, and
chow mein he brought for the mother.

As the gunman jumped in his car and raced down the
darkened streets, two questions filled my mind. How did that
young man get played so horribly by his baby momma, and
when would the police arrive? While he moaned and writhed

in pain in the middle of the street, I saw his blood spreading out underneath him, mixing into the cement.

The excitement of being a new father caused him to forget how trifling the mother was, and it took twenty five minutes for the police and paramedics to arrive, were the answers to my questions. The hospital was only four blocks away, but by the time the paramedics arrived he was dead. Unfortunately for justice, the mother had a no snitching policy.

Confrontations such as this were common, excessive. A lot of good not-taken advice led to that incident. I bet neither man knew who the father of that child really was. The new life would be fatherless and there would be no justice because a young, Black man gunned down in the street was not news.

My eyeteeth began to elongate the pull of the thirst was upon me, I've got to get out of here.

I continued my journey, looking up at the stars to hold back my tears. Vampires were different from humans. We didn't kill over pettiness, vampires had a responsibility. The vampire was an obligated creature with one hell of an appetite.

I ran from the just witnessed horror and thought of how powerful and complicated vampires were. We drank blood, but didn't want to kill. The sun burned us, but somehow fire was not a problem. The taste for blood is with us at birth, but we didn't get our powers until puberty. My nails are strong but broke from all the buildings I dug them into.

We bruised easily and healed quickly. The older we were, the longer we sleep. Sleep was how we regenerated. Any scrapes and gashes I received throughout the night would be completely healed with a few hours of sleep. Severe wounds took longer. Seeing at night was no problem for vampires. Our irises hyper dilate for better night vision. That was probably a trait left over from when there was very little light in the world. Vampires get abilities at puberty, but our powers grow after the Festival of Light, when we bonded, had a child, or became elders.

The Festival of Light, which is held in secret, had elegant halls, pillars of fire and extravagance ceremonies, but more than that it was a reminder of how we got where we were. My mother says that there are more vampires now than at any other time she could remember. My parents may one day become elders. Well, my mom might, my dad's too militant. If my performance in the Festival is good it would help her become an elder.

You wouldn't find vampires in videos taking off their clothes, chronicling viral misfortunes, or posting naked photos. Vampires have half a soul, so our images appear washed-out, faded or dull in a mirror or when captured on video.

If I had larger assets, I would highlight them. Who was I kidding? No, I wouldn't. I didn't want someone hanging out with me or talking to me because my cleavage was all up in their face or because my ass was out. Attention is good, but I was not insecure enough to be addicted to it. The Festival of Light was coming and embarrassing attention was one sure way of getting the elders to bind your powers.

My mom didn't pressure me; I put pressure on myself. That was something I picked up from my dad. "If you can see it, you can achieve it," he says. "You never know, there might be a vampire in the white house one day."

I climbed down firehouse thirty six after successfully making through streets full of screaming lunatics. There on the beach I walked along the shore with sea foam thoughts, reflecting on whether or not I should surrender to the dream.

In a world that teamed with savages, it was good that in this city there were a few other vampiric residents, but they were much older than me, so they only set off brief warnings. Vampires are not like these millionaire and billionaire Black folks who don't own as school. Vampires in positions of power are obligated to help out fellow vampire beings, it's kinda mandatory. I never ran into another vampire on my nightly flirtations.

One night each month, on a full moon a female vampire's hormone unpredictably rose and fell. Four nights a year a *Blood Moon* occurs and that is when then I would be light headed, my senses erratic, my strengths unreliable and the thirst at its highest. Those are the times when I took the stairs.

Looking down on the city was almost like looking up at the stars. It was as if the darkness was a blanket that covered the life within the city. After nightfall, buildings lit up like it was Christmas. Apartment lights on different floors flickered off and on as if the inhabitants were playing a game. I was inconspicuously present at the sudden deaths in nursing homes and hospitals. I studied on top of museums and playhouses. I ran through parks.

Skyscrapers hosted my yoga sessions. Those buildings were high, strong, and peaceful. I was alone with my heron and bow poses, alone with my thoughts. The inner city buildings were witness to my solo exercises. The energy and ambient noises usually provided background music to my movements.

Most nights, it was just the recyclers, police, homeless and me. I was an explorer not some kind of nocturnal monster. At night, it doesn't matter what your skin color was or what name brands you wore. From the highest hilltop I had a panoramic view of the city, especially at night. The city was beautiful at night, it was quieter.

The moving lights rushed down one way and then up another while half blind streets coiled their way to the heart of the city. Moving lights crisscrossed and connected boulevards, avenues, and streets. The absence of orange sodium vapor lighting darkened the roads that connected alleys and parkways. Downtown monolithic towers painted the darkness with brief dances of light as fog draped beachfront skyscrapers rose into the skyline.

Darkness laid over me like a million wants. It was in my soul. The night touched everything. I ran wild on rooftops, scurried through parks and beaches at night. I was free.

All that the night gave me was taken away by the day. In the daylight, the same downtown buildings were nothing more than blighted cement rectangles covered by glass. They look no better than grey blocks of smudge against the dull blue skyline.

For a second, my thoughts were deflected by the whirl of an electric blue bicycle. The billboards and neon signed storefronts eerily beckoned my attention, but it was the clusters of light that revealed the highest concentration of people. Those were the places where a vampire would have the most fun.

The flickering reds and blues surround me. The array of colors fit together like a perfect jigsaw puzzle. In-between blaring sirens and shotgun blasts, the night city appeared to be created by one act of inspiration instead of thousands.

From dizzying heights, I looked down at them. My teeth grew, I feel like a caged animal. I wished I had my father's ability to read minds so I wouldn't have to worry about what was thought of me. I saw them waiting at the corner, impatiently looking around, and then pressing the walk button for a fourth, fifth time. The light changed from red to green and their arms and legs swung. Me, I climbed higher.

I climbed higher than the guy lying in a gutter clutching a bottle, higher than the woman rooting through the trash, higher than the horse-play of adolescence, higher than the vomit on these stairs, higher than user views, higher than honesty, and I stayed higher than the shotgun clapping in the shadows.

I rose above unchecked homework as I moved higher than juvenile detention centers. I went higher than men that punched women, higher than the good mothers who called their daughters little bitches and tramps. I was higher than the mothers screaming they had sacrificed because they gave up drinking for three months during their pregnancy.

I climbed higher than women who put themselves into shelters so they could get Section 8 quicker. I reached higher than sobriety, higher than hungry children. I scaled higher than all the questions; higher than rogue vampires that drunk human blood. Standing on the top of the building was me getting high.

Humans learn before they could walk that their body made them special. In school, they listened to external peer voices over internal voices. They had the kind of guidance that made them spend most of their time, purchasing, taking off shirts and popping their ass to gain attention and confidence. These kids would be lucky to survive the lesson taught by their heroine and hormone filled heroes who never managed to say, "I'm sorry."

Inside Angel Beach University I crouched down by the small, manmade lake to watch the red mouths come out the water to gulp down the grapefruit pieces and Cheerios I tossed onto the surface. Soon, there were more splashes, more mouths and an assortment of flowing blue and orange fins devouring the treats I brought.

My father taught me to shoot and throw a ball, but more than that he taught me to think for myself. Out here on the edge every night what he taught me came into play. My thoughts become thought against a backdrop of miniaturize landscapes and raked white sand. When the sun went down I questioned the answers. The moonlight subtly reflected off the scales, momentarily catching my eye and causing me to recall one of my father's conversations with his friends.

"Inner-city communities are set up so the residents kill themselves," my father began. "Why else would they make allowances for these grand social experiments to take place? Everywhere you look; there are a million channels and a million sites all with same images, sex, violence, sex, violence all of it repeated. With one side of their mouth they say that those images don't have an effect, and with the other side they advertise all the products in the world.

"And, then there is the vampire. Some believe that vampirism is just evolution of the human genome, a mutation, a better one. As human society falls into decay, they use less and less of their soul. They are parasites to one another without the blood sucking benefits. The vampire drinks blood to survive. Humans bathe in blood for glory, for sport, out of sheer boredom, and this— this is known as a noble creature.

"I remember like it was yesterday when law enforcement regularly released Black prisoners into the hands of White lynch mobs and then stood by as their black bodies were hanged from trees, burned or torn to piece and given out as souvenirs. Today white arrogance and Black whining are thoroughly intertwined between excess and profit.

MG Hardie

"The human is a creature that, for no good reason, sulks
around at night just as much as a vampire. This is a creature
that kills for the thrill of it, the power of it, because it can. This
is a creature that extorts its own offspring for personal gain.
This is not a creature to admire. No, this is a creature to be
despised," he finished. He continued drinking his nectarine
vodka Collins and sat the rest of that evening in silence.

On Saturdays, aside from going with the girls on their
weekly pharmacy contraception run, I went to a lot of movies,
washed clothes, sugared and arched. I also helped my mother
clean her salon. On those days, her salon was always packed
with wearers of designer bags, shoes, and sandals. In the
morning I set out bagels and coffee. Music played while you
were shampooed, washed, and conditioned. My mother didn't
want her clients to wait for hours unnecessarily.

She took pride in getting ladies in and out in a timely
fashion. On the wall was a big screen monitor set up for
customers who needed to bring children. She treated people
how she wanted to be treated. She wanted her salon be a
getaway for women, a sanctuary, not just another place to be
disrespected and stressed.

Someone was always coming into Venus trying to sell
something at a discount or trying to whip up the ladies about
the latest racial injustice. Last week, the city councilman came
in passing out flyers. He was organizing a march. My jaw
dropped when my mother put down the flat iron, and said,
"All you do is hand out petitions while you tell us the latest
outrages. We see you every week on television; we've all been
to your website. I even voted for your ass, but even you must
realize that petitions and marches mean you have no power."

Midnight

There were always new faces mixed in with the regulars. The weekend before last, the ladies said it was a shame they never saw a nice young lady in heels. So, I tried on those four inch two leather, turquoise heels. I almost broke my neck in those hooker heels. For the record, I had never fallen in heels; I have always caught onto something before I hit the ground. When I was in the salon, I stayed quiet, poured wine and listened to the brilliant women talk about people more than school girls did.

They talked about any and everything from how a good looking man in a well fitted suit was lady-porn to expert package watching to politics. In my mother's nightly lessons, she could be quite the lecturer, but in the salon she was a woman of few words. She let her looks do the talking. Most of the single women had regrets or complained about one thing or another. The married ones agreed that they never have enough time. My mother's voiced dissents.

"Ladies, please, these are all situations that we women control. We are the ones that need to examine what and who we are spending time on and with. The most powerful thing we have as women is choice," she said as she motioned to her next client.

It was like a soap opera down there, everyone got in on the act. Most of the gossip was funny, but, sometimes things got serious. My mother demanded that everyone was respectful. "All right now," she'd scold them or she'd say, "That's not funny," in her own deadpan way.

It would have been funny had she said it.

Usually the first chair in any shop is reserved for the weakest stylist. The struggle is real for first chair stylists who also washed windows, maintained the stock room and run errands. First chairs love it when I'm was around because I do the things they didn't want to do. I saw my mom do some amazing things with hair. She was always available to help the first chair stylist, even though some of them were clearly beyond help. She does what she can; she had a reputation for beautifying even the most difficult cases.

Mom says junk food is the food you ate that makes your junk bigger, she teaching me how to cook. Each month she showed me something different, Italian, West African, but it doesn't get any better than Ivorian grilled fish and spicy sweet plantains. Mom has to go over a lot of things with me because after graduating high school, the Festival of Light is the vampire's final exam.

During the Festival, the elders tested not only your knowledge and how you assimilated, but also your speed, agility, and strength. The more I thought about it, the more I thought of the Festival as a way to unleash our natural dominant aggressions and to quell the rebel thoughts. It kept young vampire minds busy and off of our status in the human world. It pits us against each other and reinforced our place.

Young vampires weren't slaves to feeding or to sleep, so we need to have something to show for the time we spent. We had to become good vampire citizens. The elders want to make sure you were developing properly. A bad performance reflected negatively on your parents. If you passed, the elders' extended your abilities. If you didn't pass, your powers were bound; failure was not an option for me.

Humans had no idea how hard it was not to give in to the thirst. There were so many things we couldn't do. We prepared our own food because you never knew if someone put garlic in it. Most of us didn't wear jewelry because you never knew if silver was in it.

Midnight

Vampire families paid a tribute to their covens and each coven had different goal. More vampire families were heading out west. My dad told me that the covens were opening up an all vampire school. He said that discontent in the covens was growing. The school was necessary so vampires didn't have to go to school with humans.

My dad wasn't interested in getting along with humans. He wanted vampires to get along with other vampires. He is engaged in continuing to build the vampire power base. I was worried about transferring and now I couldn't think of a better place to plan my future, so when the vampire school opens in a year, I'll help my father as much as possible but I won't be attending.

I can no longer sit through movies and television shows that reduce vampires to ridiculousness. I see humans trying to eradicated our existence and retroactive holding our sins against us. In many ways my dad was right. He spoke to me of a time before light. He spoke fondly of the campaigns of Hannibal Barca, Attila, Lucius Domitius Ahenobarbus, Ivan Vasilyevich IV and François-Dominique Toussaint Louverture. He spoke of them as if he was there.

He told stories about Queens Hatshepsut, Zenobia, Wu Zetian, Makeda, Nyabinghi, and Emperor Justing II as if he were their confidant. He also carried a riveting tale of Cleitus the Black who was decapitated by his best friend, Alexander of Macedon.

Mom says integration is for the good of all. When she played the oldies, she reminisces about being in the audience as Paul Lawrence Dunbar read poetry. The yellow of her eyes subtly shined as she detailed examples of vampire integration, like Zora Neale Hurston, Bass Reeves, Jean Baptiste Point de Sable, and Ludwig van Beethoven of course, there's that whole Nat Turner incident, but vampire don't talk about that.

As I roamed the university I wondered if one day a mother will tell her vampire daughter stories about how I became the *Fangs of Fate*...

Mom and dad don't teach history they remember it. Vivid details of great battles and even greater warriors. Their recollections of colorful and strong monarchs are fascinating. When they describe it you can almost see the battle formation and hear the clashes of polished steel...

Are vampires to live in the shadows of humans forever?

About five years ago I was singing pop songs in dad's new sports car while driving around Beverly Hills. It was a great day, we were looking for a new home. We had been driving around for ten minutes when we saw the flashing lights and heard some type of yelp sound from a police car. My dad pulled over, smiled at me, and told me that everything would be okay.

I sat in that car envisioning my dad doing vampire mind tricks on him. The officer took my dad's driver's license and the car registration. After running my father's information, the officer asked what we were doing in that neighborhood.

My father smiled while the officer explained why we had been stopped. The whole time my dad was reading the officer's thoughts. He read repeated thoughts of:

I'm going to find something on this nigga. A big monkey and a little one monkey, monkeys have no business moving into Beverly Hills.

Those were the thoughts that rattled around in the officers head, but never came out of his smiling mouth. After twenty minutes, a sergeant and a K-9 unit were on the scene. They returned my father's materials. The sergeant turned to me and said, "Do you know this man?"

"My Dad?" I replied.

The officers laughed as they went back to their vehicles and left. My dad didn't start driving until they left. As the day passed, his demeanor was different. He was distant and he kept muttering about the white gods of perversion and how a Black man couldn't look for a home in Beverly Hills. He repeatedly expressed to no one in particular how lucky the officer was that he was trying to integrate.

That night after dinner, he turned to me and said, "In the shadows is where the vampire remains, disgraced before God and man. Baby girl, here, a vampire is a falcon among sparrows. There was a time when you could call someone innocent and it would be true… now no one is innocent."

At the hotel, he put on his familiar black trench coat and jumped out of the window into the night. Hours later, when he returned he went straight into the bathroom. I only heard the shower running and my dad crying. That was the first and only time I had ever heard my father cry.

The next day, the *Beverly Hills Courier* reported that the police department had burned down, several police cars were destroyed and an officer was missing. To this day, my father has never said a word about what happened. He had compromised by not killing humans. He thought the money would insulate him; he thought bigotry was all behind him. I don't think he's been the same since.

Mom made you aware she was intruding into your mind, Dad, not so much. I occasionally saw my father lost in thought or lost in someone else's thoughts. As I said, my father was a man of few words; the only thing he ever told me about love was that real love asked for nothing.

A girl wanted to be first in someone's life, my father gave me that. I mean, we were girls, if you tried to impose rules on us, we'd act like there weren't any, but there were rules to being a girl. Apparently, there were rules to being anything. Being a girl was more than clothes, hair, nails and a monthly period. It was a lot of pressure.

I called my father once a week, partially to catch up and partially to put his mind at ease. The Festival loomed large for all of us, so whenever I call him, he quizzed me.

"What have you being working on?"

"Being invisible…"

"What have you learned?"

"That guys call girls bitch and ho because that's the only kind of girl that would deal with them."

"What the hell… no! Not about humans and stop smiling Amber…"

"Oh, I learned that some vampires can command water, they can make it move faster or slower, though, we can't be in it. Some vampires can glide on the air and some can use the Earth's soil to become stronger. We are drawn to the sun, but it weakens us. The day weakens us, the night gives us strength. It has been said that the oldest elder in our coven can command ancient vampire powers."

"There is a lot more to being a vampire than learning to walk on walls and jumping on rooftops. How are you dealing with the thirst?"

"It takes some getting used to, but I think I am winning."

"Remember that fame, fortune, revenge, and ambition can rule humans every bit as much as the thirst rules us."

"Yes, sir."

"What about the Festival of Light?"

Midnight

"Every vampire that is of age must attend. Do well and your powers are given a boost, fail and you'll wish you were human."

"What else?'

"The cross and fish symbols are pagan symbols. The cross wasn't used by the religious until the fourth century. The cross is the only symbol that holds any power over vampires. The fish symbol is designed in the shape of the female sex organ and I know some sick guy thought that up. It is actually the symbol of Dagon, the god of the Philistines. I think that is in *Judges* 16:23 or was it *1st Samuel* 5:2?"

"It is in both."

"Thanks."

"Tell me about the protection symbol?"

"That's the ritual circle. It's an empty, red circle, that's why we vampires commune. Most circles with a letter or shape in them have some connection to a vampire. That includes the peace symbol, which is a broken cross within a circle, that one is obviously vampire. Ages ago, it was called the Cross of Nero. Nero believed that a world of peace could be attained if all of Christians were gone, so he killed thousands of them under that symbol."

"I love you too dad."

"I love you baby girl. Remember, you never need permission to be excellent."

"You know it..."

Over the phone, I could feel my father smiling, maybe I was projecting. He loves me, but I think he quizzes me only to see if mom was holding up her end of the bargain. My father wasn't a good dad, he's a better one. He always seemed so sure of himself. I wondered if he was ever confused growing up. Was he ever confused watching humans live their lives?

MG Hardie

Some humans exist in grey areas and tonight some of those wouldn't make it home. When vampires broke the rules, prostitutes and homeless made up large portions of victims. Some vampires kill taxi drivers and then used their vehicles to pick up unsuspecting victims. In cities all around the world, humans went missing every day.

Yesterday, I stumbled upon a body; the newly rotting odor led me to her. She lay half covered on the side of a darkened road on the Westside. I had never seen a dead body, until then. She lay there dead, face down in the dirt. She couldn't have been more than thirty. Her body was broken, her throat was slashed, and her body was drained of blood.

She was posed in a way you would think she was sleeping. Her eyes were open, but lifeless. I wasn't horrified. I just wondered if her family would miss her, did she even have a family? She looked like one of my victims from my dreams. I could tell that this was the work of a vampire. The next day the police identified the victim, but remained silent on the details. Vampires were not the only thing humans had to worry about at night.

When there were no lifeless bodies to find, I watch just shipped weapons, drugs, people get unloaded at the port. There were low flying, small planes landing in the middle of the city to offload illegal cargo to be distributed to various corner franchises around the nation. And of course there were the police extorting everyone, it all moved along pretty seamlessly. I saw everything.

Law enforcers' grabbed women and men off the street, mostly minorities, and a week later the newspapers reported them missing. They weren't really missing. They were facedown in an alley somewhere, in the trunk of a black and white, or in a landfill. It seemed to me that any organization that served the public should also be reviewed by the public it served. But, I was only fifteen. What did I know?

Look at these couples arguing again, humans just didn't know how to be happy with what they had. I kept later hours than the late night mechanic and the all-day partier. At night, nothing was predictable. My favorite prime time shows were real life. My ability to be unseen allowed me to see lives in their purest form.

One night, a suspicious fire engulfed a home on the Southside while a little girl stood on her lawn in silence clutching her burnt doll. The fire department arrived too late to save the home. The fire was suspicious because a few nights before, I overheard city officials trying to get the family to move. The family had refused the offer to move that night; tonight they had to move.

Then, there were the gangs. The impression most people had of a gang was only what the media gave them, the shootings, the fighting and the crime. They'll never see the community of a gang, the generational tradition, or how being affiliated with a gang was about survival, not criminality.

Spoon-fed humans could never see how gangs maintained order in areas that the law had trouble policing. In the parks was where I saw the gang meetings, the cash transactions, and the sex. Often I was the only witness to thefts.

I wish these thought had left me when I left the Japanese garden, but they hadn't. Found a nice spot next to a skylight on top of the University's Central Hall to lie down and look into the heavens.

How can Vampire be so civilized, and yet, we have to hide in the face of constant human brutality?

My English teacher insists on making us watching two movies in class a week. So I have taken it upon myself to learn all I can. Tonight I've read *Death of a Salesman* and *A Rose for Emily* and before I leave I'll polished off some William Carlos Williams poems.

I traveled six miles over buildings and houses to sit quietly at the beach. I loved listening to the waves brushing against the shore. I dug my feet into the still warm sand and listen to the crabs scurry across rocks. My feet were the first to feel the warmth of the sand and the first to feel the dew on the grass in the parks.

Every night, smoke, fumes, dirt, dust, garbage, gases, and other smells permeated my clothes; they needed the strongest of laundering possible. People that lived in big cities no longer breathed fresh air or saw any large, green, open spaces. They had become used to the always the deafening noise of vehicles and factories that were everywhere. Because of all the factories, industrial centers, and the overcrowding, humans were generally unhappy, no matter the situation.

Mom says humans had always been more savage than vampires, and that vampires were merely villains of convenience for our stepbrother. My mother always seemed to know the right things to say. I wondered what she would say about Adrian. What would happen if I got involved with a human? Why couldn't I just be fifteen?

Every night before she left the house she played the music and taught me about vampire history. Throughout history, vampires and humans had been enemies. She said that because of the twins, Adam and Lilith, humans and vampires would always dislike each other.

Human beings had a latent fear and hostility toward vampires and anything else they didn't understand and they really hated what they couldn't conquer. Humans only accepted creatures that were wholly subservient and submissive. For example, humans had dogs, cats, and birds for pets. They fed and cared for these pets. And, in return, they were given a subservient form of tenderness and gratefulness. Humans return that tenderness by caring for those pets and by creating laws to protect them.

The vampire was not a dog or a cat. Those animals didn't have hope, faith, or a soul, not even half of one. The vampire was the only creature that truly wanted redemption. We had a half-soul; and in every other way, we were superior to human beings. We had an equal right to exist; some believe the vampire being to be superior to the human being.

Vampires were not the kind of creature that would go quietly into the night. We integrated, but we were not a defeated, nor were we an inferior race. We would fight for our freedom, we were not pets. And let's face it any creature with two legs that carries a creature with four legs is probably not the smartest being on the planet.

In my mother's nightly lessons she seemed to know everything, but did she know that at night I hung out downtown by myself? Did she know that I often sat lonely on top of buildings? Did she know that I inhabited concrete perches from Little Cambodia to the barrios where music played all night long? Did she know that I roamed dirty ledges and viewed the lives of others through cracked windows? Did she know how many children woke up to parents yelling at each other? I did.

Did she know that every few blocks on the North Side there were ADRH's, After Drug Raided Houses? Did she know that there were parts of the city where the rats fed exclusively on perversion? Did she know that even premium bodies were on sale? Did she know that there was a price on everything, everyone? Did she?

MG Hardie

On the way home I sat above them and watched them scurry off to Kings Strip club, house party kick backs, and various booty calls. Humans had no choice but to live their lives at street level. Whether I was the third floor or the thirty-ninth, I chose not to.

Let there be midnight.

Chapter Six

When I wasn't studying, I was on the phone, drinking strawberry lemonade, or working on my basketball game. If the defender gave me a step, I finger rolled off the backboard. If they showed me any daylight, I pulled up from distance. I watered the paspalum grass in the front yard and ran basketball plays ran through my head, while the Delfonics played in the background.

My mother's garden was small, but beautiful. She took extra care with the garden. In the moonlight, the plants all seemed to turn toward her, she commanded their attention. The roses quietly gossiped when she went off on her nightly romps. The flowers appreciated the way she smoothed their beds and drew there skirts away from wild company.

Her garden was not cultivated in an accidental way. The grass edges were trimmed before they reached the concrete path. My mother nodded at me from the window as I took the trash cans around to the street. After my chores were completed, I worked on my confidence killer, the hesitation ball fake behind the back crossover...sweet.

Since arriving here, I hadn't had an urge to continue my piano lessons. My plan was to explore every nook and cranny of the city in the day and then again at night. This place is perfect because there was a shopping center every few miles. Shopping centers mean lots of activities. At night, the stupidest ideas became practical, brilliant, in fact.

MG Hardie

Tonight was no different. I sat high above the curved streets in Belmont Shore. I hid in the shadows of drunken men and women while avoiding the cured tobacco smell of the middle class. From darkened creases, I silently wondered had anyone seen me. They hardly look up from their small screens so tonight, I watch humans wander about walking their enslaved pets.

At night, I searched for meaning, meaning beyond tapping my nails against random windows. The more I searched, the more this sheltered, quiet, brown girl changed. Vampires survived by doing and saying as little as possible around humans. Vampires didn't want to just survive, we wanted to live. My father's dividing line was one of color. Adrian's was one of class, yet, he was by habit and principle, a replica of my father.

My mother had hopes and dreams for me. My father had hopes and dreams for me. And, I dreamed of something different from them. I wondered what would happen if I were to love a human. What would happen if I were to come out as vampire to those that roam the dark alleys and parks at night?

Anyone caught out on the streets at late hours were subjected to harassment or being murdered for their paycheck. That often happened because humans didn't pay attention and were simply victims of being in the wrong place at the wrong time. I saw the thugs that nightly robbed and stole, yet, they seemed so unfulfilled. The only thing the imposed eleven p.m. curfew curbed was the brutality of the thugs, not the brutality of the law.

Monica says that, all of a sudden I had a smart mouth. I did know about that, but I had been telling people exactly what was on my mind. Before this puberty thing I was never quick to flip the script on people. Maybe my edges were rounding out. Maybe it was being an active part of my dreams or the new feelings I'd been having. Whatever it was, things were different.

A million questions plagued me. Who is Amber? Was I that girl who is so sensitive that looking at me too long was sexist? Was bumping into me in the hallway a capital offense? Was asking me about my religion against my religion? Was wondering out loud about my race, racist?

Was I the type of person who blamed my grades on how much my teachers didn't like me? Was I that person who locked herself into a career that impacted me in some way as a child? Was I the kid for whom everything was about tradition and family expectations? Maybe I was the youngster that wore two hundred dollar headphones and sneakers, the one that has the latest video game consoles, yet my family languished in poverty?

Those things really don't sound like me.

Maybe I could be a gangstress, a boss bitch that held power over men and women, using my assets to get what I wanted. Was I was the straight A student who didn't have a life outside of school, or the quiet girl who only sprang to life online? Maybe I was the rapper-slash-athlete-slash-mogul-prophet. I think I could even handle being the fun time girl, that girl everyone wanted or has had.

I don't want to be any of those things.

How could I be proud of who I was and still be afraid to be who I was? How could I keep looking at myself in the mirror and be afraid to be me? I am a Black vampire of the Uhura coven. We are the first descendants of the Lilith. I descend from a long line of proud vampires. A vampire could not change what they were; they could only hide what they were.

I loved my brown skin. My skin was a signifier of where my people had been, what they had been through. Even if I were to climb high enough or run fast enough to forget, someone could look at me and have an idea of my history. Through my mother, I learned history as an African-American, history of great women and the history of my coven. I sat my school classes accepting the fact that I was surrounded by human beings.

Humans were born as sick as any vampire. I am a vampire but in this world, human beings set the standards, they made the rules. Humans were superstitions, zealots, and violent hypocrites. We vampire feared what their hatred would drive them to do. If I came out, I could be driven from school by angry students and reckless parents. I that happened to a boy on the east coast, I heard that his small clan was destroyed.

My little crew attended a city council meeting. They were voting on budget cuts that would close five recreation centers, twelve after school programs, and reduce the library hours by half. As I walked on top of the Aston Fisher Bridge, the largest bridge in Angel Beach, I reflected on our afternoon activity.

As Adrian approached the podium someone in the hall yelled out "These reforms need reforms!"

Adrian composed himself at the microphone and said, "You do this as if the pain of being a teenager isn't enough. At Angel Beach High, thirty two students have dropped out, six have lost their lives in shootings, and others have overdosed. We have to deal with good teachers, bad teachers, and those that want to touch on you. Outside of school, the police want to lock you up, and on your way home you have to dodge the hoochies and gangstas.

"And, this council wants to cut programs that help latch key kids and single parents. You condemn us, but you are the ones that are closing rec centers and making these cuts. We are the victims, what outlets do we have? Some teenagers are delinquents, but look at their parents, they're a mess. They are uninvolved and abusive. They are not even equipped to be in charge of another life form. So, how do you expect children to learn in an environment like that?

"The only reason you act like being a teenager is criminal is because we can't vote and because you remember all the hell you caused as teenagers. With you, it is always the way we walk, the way we talk, the way we act, what we listen to, who we are with, how we dress. You don't give a damn about how we think or how we feel. You ignore us, and then talk about how bad our homework is and complain about how we don't read.

"You see, our generation has to lie down in the street as though we're dead. Is this the only acceptable position for our young bodies? Have you all forgotten how scary the world is to children? Have you forgotten what it is like to experience things for the first time? Have you forgotten going to bed confused by it all? You deride our music when there was a time when it was your music that was derided. You have all done something that you swore you would never do, you've turned into your parents.

"These kids aren't all getting high, having sex, and hanging out. If you just took a few seconds, you would realize that most of us are still finding ourselves. We seek fellowship with others like us. We seek comfort in groups, but that doesn't mean we are in a criminal enterprise. We aren't all rule breakers and rebellion, piercings and tattoos, big butts and rock hard abs. If look, if you really look, you will find that some of us are just like you...fighting every day.

"If you pass these cuts, what options are you leaving us? I am pretty sure that most of you don't even care because your children attend private schools. You can't even see us, we don't exist and still you just want to control us. When will the nation mourn for us? When will we be too big to fail?"

There was a moment of silence as he stood there calmly in front of the city council. The applause from the crowd allowed the members to pick their collective jaws off the floor. I suppose I wasn't the only one to fall in love with him at that moment.

He's a light on the dark side of me. He was passionate and articulate, I loved that about him. The city council commended him and five minutes later, the budget cuts passed. No one paid attention to children until they did something drastic. Children had no credibility

After the budget cuts passed, the hall cleared. Adrian smiled, looked at us and said "What is a speech going to do when you run out of options? We all need to be a part of something bigger, something outside of ourselves." Those were the moments I forget to breathe around him. I wonder if he knows that he has me.

At the council meeting words seemed to smoothly tumble out of his mouth. When I was not lost in the cut of his jaw line, his voice or simply watching the majestic way he walked, I listened to him talk about the world and what was needed in the community. He moved me to attend the Lives Matter rallies with him. He moved me to leave then when they got off-task and complained about the disconnected polysyllable use of Black intellectuals. It really didn't matter, I loved watching him breathe.

In Angel Beach, there were fifty-five gangs, or cliques, or whatever the media is calling them. Some of them danced, some skated, some ride bikes, and not all of them are violent. Our youth forces us to pay attention to how a singer looks before how they sound. We look at shit and have no idea what we are looking at. We pay more attention to how we look with another person, instead of how that person makes us feel. We pay attention to how someone began, and not who they are.

We would never figure out on our own that the parts of the city with worst pollution are also the ones that had the most crime. We virtually pit artists against each other instead of appreciating their individual talents. We couldn't comprehend how the accumulation of non-sense, hits and the weight of abuse could cause someone to snap.

We didn't follow doctorates to protests, we followed reverends. You couldn't pay us to believe the links between video images and body chemistry. We kids learned early on that rewards would be given for those with a readiness to lie. We knew everything, and we did all those freaky things to him just to outlast the other hoes.

We run around trying to build a brand instead of building ourselves. We couldn't sit still long enough for you to explain how much profit was being made from the deaths of youth. We wear clothes that read Harvard and couldn't locate the state it was in. We had London, Milan, and Paris on our half-tops, but couldn't find those cities on a map to save our lives. We were not into virtue, modesty, or details, we are all about sensations. Adrian didn't front, he was a real SJW, Social Justice Warrior.

Angel Beach is a suburb of Los Angeles County, which is one of the largest cities in the world. In it you could find anything from brush lands littered with double sized trailer parks to filthy hick bars under the shadow of the County's mountain range to the neon-splashed refuge of movie star wannabes. The county had everything from abandoned factories to jacking cars to well kept hedges to littered streets. It had subway and bus lines on one side and sky walk-ways on the other.

One of the first pueblos in California was *El Pueblo de la Reina de Los Angeles* because of its proximity to the water—*El Plays de Nuestro Senora La Reina de Los Angeles*, the Beach of Our Lady the Queen of Angels. Both the city and the beach were named in honor of the shrine found in Assisi in Italy to the Virgin Mary, *Santa Maria degli Angeli*—"Our Lady of the Angels."

On the coast of Los Angeles County was Angel Beach, which was basically an urban-Americana theme park. "The Beach" as we called it was an orderly tangle of small towns within a larger city. Four highways cut through it, creating thousands of intersecting streets that separate various areas. The sane were still crazy and the city was just as untamed as anything else.

North Angel Beach was ruled by gangland graffiti, acts of pure vandalism, low rent, and lower morals. West Angel Beach was dominated by housing projects, industrial areas, oil refineries and tanker storages. East Angel Beach was populated by boarded-up shops, tatty slat-board houses and old cannabis smells. Downtown had direct access to the freeway as clusters of skyscrapers rose around city hall as the city's homeless intermingled alongside businesspeople.

Midnight

Surfside was like the name says. Fishing, surfing, gliding, jet skiing; if it had anything to do with the water, you could do it there. The Marina contained multimillion dollar party boats and sea lions. It was also a hive of new age playboys and swim-suited pin-ups.

Belmont Shore was a small stretch of land right by the beach. It was filled with condos and homes that had amazing scenic views of the ocean. Naples and Belmont Shore framed opposing sections of shoreline drive. The Golden Peninsula was where the retired wealthy went to live out the rest of their days.

California Heights, Angel Hills, and Signal Hill uncomfortably rested as middle class buffers between East and North Angel Beach. A state college set between Golden Peninsula and Seal Beach. The junior college was close to North Angel Beach and Lakewood. West and North Angel Beach was where most of the black comedy occurred. All of those areas were a part of Angel Beach, but they each had their own police and fire departments.

There was always a handful of television shows being filmed in the city every day. There were at least ten large festivals and a grand prix held in the city every year. In a month, there would be a winter celebration on Christmas Tree Lane. The beach extended about ten miles, the conflict between the have and have nots extended far longer. There was a huge aquarium and several ocean bays, not to mention the port.

I lived in East Angel Beach, one of the many subdivided neighborhoods along with Angel Hills. The Eastside had its share of psychopaths, deviants, and crude restaurant signs daubed on sheet metal. The city was about an hour from just about every major Southern California attraction and theme park. Next to Angel Beach were the smaller cities of Rancho Palos Verdes, Newport Beach, and a host of other beach named cities. The 405 freeway was the concrete backbone of all of those cities.

Each of my friends lived in different sections of the city, so before I went out I checked to see if Tiff, Holly, JD, or Los would be able to stalk around with me. I didn't let a day go by without messaging them. I knew they couldn't come out, but that was what friends were for.

Carlos was Salvadoran. He had a large family and there were always little kids running around his house. Los didn't talk about it, but his father didn't live with them. When I saw his father, I thought he was a mechanic because he was in dirty coveralls and had grease under his fingernails. It was pretty gross.

Both his mother and father are undocumented, so they have to deal with things Carlos will never understand. Every now and then his mother would yell, Espanol! She demanded that he spoke Spanish to her and right after she did, he encouraged his siblings to speak English when I was around. In her accented way, his mother used to call me, 'Chor friend.'

"Is dis chor friend from school? Is chor friend helping you study? Is chor friend staying for dinner?" I asked her for more of her atole de elote, which was awesome by the way, and that was when she began calling me Amber.

Being homosexual is only a big deal for family members; Carlos says most people just don't live up to their avatars. He's webmaster to a ProAna site, an anorexic lifestyle site. He pays for things with digi-currency. He doesn't push his reality on anyone and he's usually in front of as many screens as possible.

Midnight

When I first started coming by his house he couldn't scramble eggs, but now the boy can burn. He says I am his personal taste tester. I love it when me makes something called carne asada con chimol. We eat in the dining room underneath a small blue and yellow woven Dios, Union, Libertad placard.

In his house there's a visible crucifix in every room, including the bathroom. It was kind of creepy the first time I saw the *Dios te está mirando* sign over the bathroom door...if his mother only knew. Most Salvadorian dishes don't require garlic; the dishes were great without it. I spend a lot of time at Carlos' house eating, which was probably why I've gained weight so quickly.

For teenagers, how many people crushing on you was a sign of status, even some of the homeless people had someone to love them in the shadows. Carlos was the only one in our clique that didn't have someone he was digging, well, someone not digital. He expressed himself as homosexual, he seemed asexual to me. He was a virtual-lifer. He spent much of his non school hours existing in virtual reality games.

Calso lives by the code. If a hot, new game came out, we might not see him for a week. He also edited all of JD's slacklining videos and he was quite the hactivist. He turned a social disability into an advantage. Every time I saw him, he had bags under his eyes and looked exhausted. He was always going on about some app or video games.

Daily, I watched Jonathan gossip and stuff his face with junk food. Besides knowing all the gossip, he only came out of his shell when he was slacklining, which he was very good at, or when he was hunting the latest collectable sneaker. Hiding behind his talkative nature was a desire to be needed. He was always willing to take a chance when it came to freshly updating gossip, but even he couldn't chill with me during my midnight romps.

His family had a big house, but we hardly went there when his parents were home. I believed his parents thought we were dating or something because whenever I was around, they yelled something in Vietnamese at him. I wished I could read their minds. My dad says that being able to read thoughts ended friendships quickly. JD said it was nothing and I had to accept that.

JD has two younger brothers, they're twins and they were quite ingenious. The week before, I saw them install working turn signals to a shopping cart. He is third generation Vietnamese-American, so he was going to run into trouble, especially with his parents. They criticized the way he spoke Vietnamese and he challenged their rules. He was particularly agitated because his father wore white socks and flip-flops to Open House. His parents didn't understand him and he didn't want to understand them. They weren't born eight thousand miles apart but it seemed like it.

When I was with Carlos and Jonathan, I saw up close how fragile the human condition was. When I was with Holly and Tiffany, I mostly wondered would it be like to have a real girlfriend, one who knew all of my secrets.

Everyone is asleep, and I am alone on this bridge swamped by desire.

I scurried to the top of the health club and then jumped from roof to tree to the top of the police station. I sat in the darkest spot on the rooftop. My heart rate slowed as I watched the downtown buildings bite into the night. I lay on my back and slowly ran my hands down my stomach. I loosened my skirt and allowed my fingers to crawl underneath my cotton panties.

I dented the air conditioner as my black, kitten heeled booties dug into the top of the roof.   There was the sensitive spot. I touched it awkwardly with one finger, and then steadied by two fingers. The thirst subsided and then increased as my teeth descended. Cotton pressed against the back of my hand as I reaching further, feeling wetter. My soft moans drifted through the streets.

There's something about the way he looks at me, the way he talks to me, the way he feels when I touch him.

What I felt on top of that police station was more intense than crossing my legs, and rocking back and forth while reading. It was more satisfying than riding a bike or squirming in my Chemistry class seat. The muscles in my thighs tightened. I could feel the pleasure.

For the first time, I think, I think, I think I found myself.

I could feel myself being made whole. My moans turned into an echoing scream of conclusion as I snapped several antennas as breath sat heavy up the cold air. My energy increased, and for me the feeling would last all week. I dusted myself off, my steps were lighter as I continued to explore on my way home.

I could tell how much a person weighed by the sound of their footsteps. I felt powerful when I walked behind someone and they walked faster than their heart beats, and I could hear that, too. I made a sound and they looked back. I rushed by them like the wind, they crossed the street. I liked raising the hairs on the back of necks.

Chapter Seven

After months of hiding in shadows I saw what forced population migration was. It turned downtown Angel Beach into mostly condo complexes and corporations. The city had authorities forcibly moving the homeless, while public officials evicted families in the middle of the night. Old Mom & Pop storefronts were now prime locations for national franchises. The city council had been changing zoning laws and tax rules to make it more appealing for high priced condos and corporations.

I traveled all over the city, but I often sat overlooking downtown. I loved how the warm rising breeze from the Pacific Ocean to caressed my skin. In the early morning, on the opposite side of town, sometimes I saw Rick Johnson, Adrian's best friend, walking home from his job. Rick worked on the outskirts of town cleaning industrial waste off of leaking containers.

When Rick was three years old, his father started serving a twenty year prison sentence. When he was seven, his twelve year old brother was gunned down in a drive-by shooting. After the funeral, his mother got strung out on heroine, she was useless after that. At nine, child protection services stepped in and gave him to his grandparents, who routinely beat the brakes off of him. He wilded out and started hustling until he was kicked out of their house at thirteen. Two years ago he was homeless, sleeping on storefronts and in back alleys.

MG Hardie

I envied the way Rick and Adrian interacted. They knew
each other well. They had known each other since pre-school.
Two years ago when Rick was at his lowest point, Adrian was
the only person who saw hope in him. He saw redemption
and reached out his hand to him. Those two were like peas in
a pod; they told each other what they needed to hear when
they needed to hear it.

*Adrian describes me as 'an attitude with a short fuse', but
Rick says I am a 'calming force' around them, and I like that.*

Rick had a neat goatee and almost a full mustache, he
looked grown. He had never been a puppy; he had always
been a dog. He was imposing, he could play linebacker or
power forward if he wanted to, but staying alive took
precedence in his life. Being on his own required that he
learned to fight to survive, not play games. He didn't speak a
lot, but when he did, he didn't waste words. You could tell he
had really been through some shit. He had a job that he went
to almost every night.

I never saw Rick without a camera in his hand. His story
was all the way tragic, but I have never heard a negative word
come out of his mouth. Things were tough for him, but he
refused to drop out of school. They say that hanging out on
the corner is gangsta, but that ain't gangsta. You'll get stripes
for disrespecting others, downing your own, selling drugs,
fighting over hoods, leaving your child without a father, and
indiscriminately shooting at people, but that ain't gangsta.
Rick was gangsta. I mean, what was more gangsta than
working a job after school to survive?

Midnight

Insects made way for me, birds issued sporadic warnings of my approach, cats and dogs eased away in fear—animals were such alarmist. On Sundays, there were dozens of bike trails and a few ranch areas to explore. Some of those trails you could hike or you could ride a horse. Horses became especially agitated around me. It was probably because horses saw in grey, so to them, I probably looked like a walking shadow.

If mom and I weren't on one of our Sunday morning drives, I sat near a church and listen to the choirs sing hymns. After church, I rode the blue line metro rail to Los Angles. The metro rail was a rapid transit system that ran for two hundred miles. It connected parts of Los Angeles City with the other parts of the county. Once downtown, a person could go to UCLA, USC, Universal Studios, The Getty Center, the Watts Towers, Venice Beach, the Griffith Observatory, anywhere.

I watched humans get on and off the train. I made note of where they got off, what they had on, what they talked about and how they treated each other. My observations helped me paint a picture of the world and its inhabitants. The metro rail had its share of ne'er-do-wells also, but there was a lot of talent to be seen in the singers, mimes, and performers.

I was not driving so I had no problem riding the bus. I actually liked riding the bus. I loved the view and seeing all the different faces. Sometimes, the bus ride was long and solitary; sometimes, it was packed and brief.

Unfortunately, poorly raised individuals held people hostage with their loud cell phone conversations. It was hard to avoid perverts and juvenile delinquents that also rode the bus. Robbers, barbiturate users, robo trippers, tweekers, and the hypes all piled into a slow rolling metal tube. Not a good mix. In school, at least you had the choice to hang with the dregs or not, on the bus you didn't have a choice.

Watching the media you would think that boys created all the havoc, but girls were far wilder than their male counterparts. We sugar and spice females were usually afforded more passes than we actually deserved. Gangs were fronted by males, but don't get it twisted, most gangs are run by females. Most guys wouldn't do anything thing if there wasn't a female behind it. And, make no mistake; those girls were tougher than rolling a hard six. I just couldn't hang out with most of girls, they embarrassed me.

Girls not only hold your secrets against you, but they loudly bragged about having unprotected sex. Ridding bare back, raw, no rubber, just tosses away the whole concept behind Mood Condoms. I wasn't the one, Sexually Transmitted Diseases in vampires were always worse than in humans.

Most girls hardly talked about their home life or school unless it was about who they wanted to cut or slap. Of course, there were always a few females lying just to fit in. I didn't need my head filled with manifestations of their sickness; I got enough of that from popular music. I didn't have time to follow friends or copy the latest trend. My hands were full just being a teenager; a freakum dress was not an option.

I spent plenty of time looking at myself and my outfits in any mirror I could find. It wasn't as if I didn't worry about my hair and nails; I just didn't obsess over them. I had been doing my hair since I was ten. It grew fast, after a week I could cut it off again. These people spent half the day beaming info and being overly concerned with their brand, even if their brand was fucked up. I tried to not judge people. I gave those who I didn't want to be around the side-eye and then I would slide out.

Midnight

I stayed away from those girls that seemingly strived for new low scores. You know the ones that spent countless time keeping track of their men. They didn't want to be loved, they wanted to be adored. Manipulation was their only motivation for getting up in the morning.

They were the silent ones and the ones you heard saying, "Give me money," and "Ain't nothing free." What girl didn't like nice new clothes? But giving up ass for shopping sprees and spa treatments—I'll pass. Most of them only saw dollar signs and where principles should hang, they hung price tags. Bottom line; don't give her your heart when all she wants is a purse.

I never heard about good relationships, only the love-hate ones. And please, don't give these chicken heads any alcohol because they would straight fuck. Anyone that appeared to be balling could get it. For some of them, it was as if they were hurt by sobriety. They thought it was the business to be shit-faced; they ranked those alcoholic episodes and then questioned what was wrong with everyone else.

They injected, they popped, they drank, they inhaled, and they smoked away the night. They wanted to forget that the month, the week, or the night before ever happened, but they knew it did. The amnesia they prayed for never came to comfort them and they'd do it all again next week. They never learned or had someone teach them how to work with someone; most of those girls would end up being women who never had a successful relationship. It wasn't just the poor girls or the rich ones, it was all of them.

Most of them wouldn't escape their situation; they would still be talking about how they used to bounce and twerk it twenty years from now. Their expertise was in ass horizontology and they'll be sexually used up in a few years and won't even know it. I wasn't knocking their hustle or that you-only-live-once attitude because everybody can't ho, and there are such things as nice hoes.

I was as friendly as the next girl; I couldn't have people just touching all over me. I don't play that. I was not one of those simple bitches. I respected myself, my family, and my history way more than that. Besides a girl has to leave some things to the imagination, right?

With so much riding on life, why call it having game or getting played? I can't understand why humans have casual relationships. Love was a commodity that was too precious to waste, like time. I had bigger problems such as the lock on my locker only working every other day, or the fact that I was now having waking visions. Taking substances that made me touchy-feely, drinking lean, getting high on butter, or fighting over some dude that didn't want me would only make my existence worse. Yet the girls wondered how they went from main chick to sidepiece in a weekend, ain't nobody got time for that.

He was never committed to you, but you were mad and wondering why he's not committed to the child. If it weren't so damaging, it would be comical. How those silly broads could, on a daily, be concerned with the size of a guy's penis was beyond me. My mother says that love made everything better.

Love makes everything better... If I said what I just wrote to the stupid bitch network, they would probably call me old fashioned and laugh at me. No bitch, it's just not your fashion. I might be a vampire, but I was not stupid.

It wasn't enough that I had to live in this human world, but I had to be thought prude because at least six people hadn't felt me up yet. You could only avoid that teenage custom if

Midnight

you were a lesbian. Some girls were only lesbian because in this society, it was safer. In the teenage world, you were considered a square if you didn't play sip-sip-pass in the back of the bus or at someone's house. These compulsory exercises all had to be independently verified, of course.

It was three a.m. and I was running and jumping from building to building on my way home. I was alone with my thoughts. Los is right, life is all about choices. A person chooses to allow their body to be a party. They chose to be a hoodrat. We kids always claim we don't want a relationship, but all we wanted was a relationship. We all wanted to know each other. In every school, kids made out with each other, fondled each other behind bleachers, or felt each other up at parks.

The city was so large that a little girl could get easily lost, a *little* girl... not me. I just counted the number of dirty alleys, dead ends, and streets littered with plastic bottles, and before you knew it, I was home. I could also follow the discarded soda cans and old lottery tickets, or I could simply follow the scent of old meth labs. I left the curved streets and hidden schools, and returned to darkened avenues where every other street light was out. Some parts of town were so beat up that roaches rode rats like horses.

Law enforcement liked to keep the murders, shooting, break-ins, and robberies on the north side, but those offenses were in every section of town. My favorite place to go was Hilltop Park; it was in the middle of the city, the highest point on Angel Hills. Before curfew, it was usually populated with teenagers that smelled like a fifth of everything. After midnight, I went there to get a complete view of the city. I exhaled. My vampire powers were growing. I soaked it all in as my world was changing.

For me, it was a rush setting off alarms at the aerospace company that was at the far end of town. Of course, I had no interest in secret government projects, but toying with state of the art surveillances system was a good way to test how stealthy I could be, and it beat the hell out of charting sentence trees. Emergency sirens were in the distance as I went up another fire escape. I saw my block, I was almost home.

When I prowled around at night, I debated within myself whether or not to intervene in a robbery, should I help someone get home safely. The lights on the Vincent Thomas Bridge flickered as I dangerously walked on top of it.

My abilities are growing. Am I wasting them?

Those flickering lights caused my mind drifted back to last night's lesson…

"The collective reality of people smiling and posing for lynching photos is evidence that these beings are not animated by justice," Mom began. "Humans have historical amnesia. They are out of control, nothing shames them. From crossing an ocean to enslave to escaping elite slave masters, humans need little excuse to kill humans and even less to kill vampires. The fact is that more Europeans settled in the north because they couldn't compete with the slaves in the south, not out of righteousness."

Then she mentally shared horrible images of helplessness during Hurricane Katrina. I wasn't sure before, but I am sure now this lesson upset me the most…

Midnight

My thoughts were interrupted by the low flying ghetto bird
as I arrived home. I don't know how children studied at night
with police helicopters constantly circling. I had just finished
Fantasia and was in a Tori Kelly mood when this thing
vibrated everything within a mile radius.

Police helicopters are the single loudest thing in the night
sky. I know they weren't drawn to the cut of the dress,
probably more reports of rooftop disturbances; I need to be
more discreet. The light from the helicopter chased only
shadow and rumor. I arrived at home silently with many
things on my mind.

Endlessly running, hands tracing my body, my fangs, the
growls, darkness— this sucks, even in my dreams I am alone.
My old friend, the dream, once again woke me up in time for
school. I was beginning to feel more and more out of place in
these nightmares where everyone is dead.

Adrian led the young adult Sunday school class. After all,
you got more education in Sunday school than in Sunday
service. I guess that was why they called it school. At
homecoming, I was surprised that he invited me to
Thanksgiving dinner at his house. The Renzors had a nice
house. They had vintage religious oil paintings hanging on the
living room walls. The paintings were of the Last Supper and
of Jesus healing the blind man.

While everyone was in the backyard playing and watching
football, Adrian gave me the nickel tour, which ended in his
room. His bedroom was what I expected, trophies and sports
equipment. What I didn't expect was a painting easel and
paintings on the wall.

His paintings of the city, the night sky had playful, vibrant
subversion to them. He also had interesting paintings of
Benjamin Franklin wearing a pulled down Dodgers cap,

MG Hardie

Ernest Hemmingway wearing sagging pants while eating eggrolls and Susan B. Anthony doing a motorcycle wheelie in a tight leather catsuit. His family was nice, even though his father stared at me for most of the dinner. I hope that was because I always turn down offers of food and not because he hadn't seen me at church service.

I had been trying to make something happen between myself and Adrian, anything. After Thanksgiving, he asked me to attend a church service, and I did. I was very uncomfortable though. I wasn't uncomfortable because the pastor's family and their guests had to sit in the front row underneath the scowl of Pastor Renzor.

It was uncomfortable because I had to sit in a church underneath portraits of white Jesus. They call this a black church, but as far as I know, the church has never been Black. His sermon was on grace. Amazing Grace was still ringing in my ears an hour later

Adrian invited me on a Sunday church trip to Disneyland. Of course, I accepted. I had never been to an amusement park. It was like a date, only it wasn't. Daylight, loud noises with running and screaming humans all over the place... and me with no filler, it should be interesting.

I had my fill of blood and left the house. Twenty of us rode the church bus to Anaheim. Disneyland was a huge amusement park and I was in awe of it. As we arrived, I heard the sounds and the screams coming from the rides and attractions, and I was anxious. It may not be a good idea strapping me into something so close to humans.

Talk about having butterflies, but Adrian was always near. I listened to him talk as we got on smaller rides, the railroad coaster, and the haunted mansion. The lines were smaller for those rides. I hugged Minnie Mouse and shook Goofy's hand. I met all of the Disney characters. I enjoyed listening to the conversations of people talking, most of which I could understand.

There were people from around the world there. It was the only place I had seen that was more international than Angel Beach High, all of it stimulated me. After all, why was I scared? Adrian didn't ask me on the trip to spin around in a little tea cup.

"Let's do it," I said as I pulled him toward Space Mountain.

We strapped in and the ride slowly started. My heart pounded, boom, boom. The track slowly clacked and then everything went dark. Adrian let out a howl. Howls, glowing lights, quick turns, my teeth began to descend. Without knowing it, I slid next to him during one of those turns and held his hand during one of those drops. It calmed me and I howled right along with him. The ride was amazing.

After two and a half minutes, the ride was over and I finally managed to catch my breath. I looked at him, and said, "So, which ride is next?" He smiled at me and off we went to another six rides. In between the scrumptious crab cakes and giant cinnamon roll, I had the time of my life. He held my hand on every ride and I made sure I slid as close as possible to him on every sharp turn. The fantasy from the attractions to the color and design of the buildings was magical.

I learned a lot about Adrian, aside from painting, he hated horror films. He liked long, slow walks in the sun. He was the only person I knew that liked to play board games. He preferred to talk in person. He actually looked me in the face and not at my breasts when I was speaking. Strangely, his favorite color was heather red. I liked the way he used his fingertips to slowly write his name on my back. He says that stretch marks were sexier than tattoos and most importantly, he says that I am special.

On the way back to Angel Beach, I was famished, everyone was laughing and talking, but it all seemed distant. I needed blood and a change of clothing. I ran into the house, gulped down some deer blood, and headed straight for the bathroom. I let the steam from the water filled the bathroom until my imaged faded from view. Right now I felt as weak as I do when he stares at me with those light hazel eyes.

Falling, being choked, lips pressed against mine, warm blood running down my mouth— a new dream has arrived to keep me company. In this dream I was an active participant.

When I awoke, my twenty-three paired chromosomes were ablaze. Puberty arrived with a vengeance, turning on my vampire DNA. For vamps, puberty lasted about three years. The first few months of this puberty thing had been nauseating. It had been filled with plenty of discoveries and even more patience. All of that was made worse by human teenagers getting turn't up and turned out.

For my Christmas gift, Adrian painted a colorful mural of my name above my bed. It gave my red walls life. While he painted, I asked him, "If all people gang up at some point, why aren't they viewed as gang members?"

He stopped painting, was silent for a moment, and said, "Because street gangs are not sanctioned by the law. White and minority gangs exist at the same time, doing much of the same things. It's the minority group that is the focus of public concern.

"Why is hanging out together wearing colors, having secret handshakes, and intimidating names okay for a sports team, but makes anyone else suspicious? Those institutions are legitimized by taxes, and that sanctions them. These laws are designed to prohibit the tax-free organizing of people.

"The police don't gun down people wearing smocks, suits, or uniforms do they? A gang is often recognized by skin color, but kids know gangs by other names. Names like club, sorority, clique, political party, coalition, officer, frat, crew, military, department, and corporation.

"Those gangs have colors, claim areas, have institutions and symbols, they have a code and, sometimes, they get together to menace others. Tax is a fee that allows them to be viewed differently than a street gang would. Gangs are the necessary results of people getting together to express themselves. Brutalizing others is what America does best. America's gangs affect children the most.

"Power is expressed through institutions and you see those leaders dealing with social issues by talking. Adults debate as long as can before they give up a small token of a solution, which is another way doing nothing. It doesn't matter if a person is white, black, green, or red... pain is pain. Every day the dominate culture ransacks our culture for fortune and fame and at the same time criminalizing the very people who provided the inspiration.

"You can't institutionalize the streets, but they sure are trying," he said as he finished off the lemon tea and continued to paint over my headboard.

None of the men in my life would ever be caught in intentional pastels and they were like nine degrees of cool, especially Adrian. The more time I spent around him, the more I started to view law enforcement racially. I had concluded that the word 'street' was just a marker of intolerance, like so many other words.

The word street meant the lack of institutional backing. The word street was used to dismiss the ethnic, religious, and often racial reasons people gathered together. The word gang didn't mean gang at all. The word gang was simply a place holder for the word youth. How humans could be led to all of the obviously wrong conclusions was beyond me.

As he painted, it was obvious that the pressure from his grades, basketball, and family expectations were on his mind. He feared failure and it was that fear that drove him more than anything else did. I was afraid of being alone. A vampire's worst fear is spending hundreds of years alone. Not drowning, not decapitation, being alone.

I can't even describe how I felt around him. It was not the energy surge I felt after breakfast. It was not the affection and respect I felt about mom and dad or my new friends. What was happening to me was not how I saw things play out in the movies. I had never felt this way before. I didn't think anyone in the history of the world had ever felt this way before. It was killing me, but it felt so right.

The basketball court was the one place I didn't feel awkward and somehow the bouncing ball pounded out my thoughts. I spent so much time patrolling the city and playing basketball that my energy levels were no longer unsustainable with a glass of deer blood. Blood made it easier for me to focus; I was more efficient, quicker, stronger... changes to my diet had to be made. I returned back to school just in time for Geometry.

Geometry class was when I usually felt fully replenished. My teacher, Mr. Sebastian, was a tall, thin, white man with aged white hair and blue eyes. He was the formal type, he always wore a full business suit and dress shoes. That was the only class I had where my seat was in the back.

Midnight

"Today, we will be discussing the Pythagorean Theorem," Mr. Sebastian said as he walked over to the blackboard and wrote $a^2 + b^2 = c^2$. The theorem was simplicity and beauty that could be seen at a glance.

Many students struggled with math. Math was pretty easy once you realized that all the numbers were connected. I was fascinated by puzzles, logical paradoxes, and perpetual motion machines. History was full of nincompoops, boneheads, ridiculous kings and queens, paranoid political leaders, compulsive voyagers, ignorant generals that fill the flotsam and jetsam of historical currents. The people who radically altered history, the great scientists and mathematicians, were seldom mentioned, if at all. They were to be admired.

I tried to remain focused on the subject, but my mind drifted off, and before you knew it, I was in the Bahamas in a tight green bikini running on Cove Beach. It was a pleasant thought that was interrupted by flashing images and dark storm cloud.

"You are vampire," said a voice in my head.

"Who are you?" I asked.

Being a young vampire at the strangest times I could feel my incisors descending. That usually occurred when I was daydreaming, and it was one of those times.

"I am the voice of Queens Eyleuka, Meresankh, Nzinga M'Bandi, and Verónica. I am the voice of those who came before..."

"Why have you come to me?" I pleaded with the voice. My head pounded. My heart beat faster. My forehead glistened. I was sinking deeper...

"You come from a long line of royalty."

"Why have you come?" I asked.

"The human... Feelings that possess, feelings that bind, feelings of lust, feelings of love. Guard your half-soul..." The voice went from a loud roar to a whisper, and faded away. "Guard your vampire heart..."

I opened my eyes. My forehead and palms were sweaty. The vision seemed like it was only a few seconds, but according to the clock, forty-five minutes had passed. I looked around the class and saw students dutifully listening to Mr. Sebastian's lecture.

New thoughts swirled through my mind as the bell rang and ended Mr. Sebastian's lecture. The students filed out of the classroom and into the hallway like a river flowing into the pre pubescence. I was on my way to my last class of the day, English with Ms. Tucker, in the bungalows on the far side of school. I opened my locker and with a loud bang, hit my shoulder on door. I was totally preoccupied with the vision.

I saw language as an art form. The letters and words were the substance and the grammatical rules were the structure. The substance and structure made up the fundamentals of any language. I wrote down my thoughts and observations as Ms. Tucker continued to talk about verbs. I received a message from Adrian asking me if I planned to go to the end of the year barbecue.   *Yes*, I messaged back, and I no longer cared about transitive verbs.

Ms. Tucker's began her lecture and I nodded off. I, again, heard the whispers.

"Remember, remember, remember... who and what you are..."

When I opened my eyes, Ms. Tucker's English lecture was over and I was the only one still sitting in my seat. The voices

Midnight

had pulled me from the human world back into the vampire one.

Okay, you've got to get a grip.

I felt half-human, half-vampire, and all Amber. There was an unbridgeable chasm dividing vampires from humans, us versus them, self against other. I didn't even feel like a vampire. I didn't feel like a human. I didn't know what to feel.

I drifted through the rest of my day and basketball practice. After my mother awoke from her slumber, I told her what happened and she explained to me that the voices were a fundamental part of vampire culture and tradition. However, I was less than forthcoming about what the voice actually said.

She turned Nina Simone down and hugged me tight. She said that the visions were 'vampire echoes'. Before I went out for the night, she told me that the echoes were a way to connect the past with the present. The echoes allowed vampires from the past to communicate and pass along knowledge, the visions were messengers.

In the day time, old people sat on stoops, loud kids ran around, and every other car blasted music. I saw that many older Blacks were asked to look the other way and now I, a Black vampire, was asked to hide while looking the other way. The thought was all kinds of sickening.

I wanted to ignore the pull of my ancestors. I wanted to ignore everything I've been told, but I wondered how it would feel not to have to hide. Humans had caused the vampire to be viewed as a perpetual bad actor. The full-soul creatures spread their sickness while the vampire masqueraded. My eyes couldn't hide my anger, but the thought of his hands touching my face caused my growing anger to subside.

MG Hardie

My nights started to bleed into one. I stayed in the streets, but I also chilled with my girls going over class work and talking. We got together and laughed for hours about silly things, watched videos, played games, and streamed shows that beeped out words that our minds put back in, but I always ended up on top of a building somewhere. I loved hanging out and talking to them, but they couldn't and wouldn't challenge the curfew. I took Tiffany to one of the buildings that I liked to haunt.

We climbed up the fire escape, but even her militancy wouldn't allow her pass the fifth floor. The police helicopters, the yelling of ill-equipped mothers, the screams of abused children, the drunken fights, and the smell of it all was just too much for her. It was so funny; I thought she was going to have a panic attack.

My mom had her friends and they were probably drinking the nightly special at the blood-bar. I was resigned to the fact that my friends would not be available to help me take back the night. One night Adrian took me up on my offer to bight roam the city. Adrian and I hopped over a railing and took the fire escape to the west end of a building.

"I don't know how you can climb these stairs so fast," he said as we went up. The path narrowed and the shoddy building construction became evident. He lost his footing on some loose masonry and I quickly grabbed his wrist as several bricks took their time falling to the ground below before exploding into powder on impact.

He grabbed the railing, used his hands to steady himself, and sighed. He was game, but he wasn't happy. He fared better than anyone else, but none of my friends were available after midnight. For us, morning came too soon.

Chapter Eight

Today my usual glass of blood didn't brighten my mood.
Last night fired raged in Angel Beach. Two churches were set
on fire; they were burned to the ground. Three people were
killed in one church and two in the other. One victim was a
seven-year-old girl.

Tiffany and I sat under the lighthouse on those stone
benches and just cried. We cried for ten minutes, I hadn't
cried this much since coming to Angel Beach. I cried for this
and another reason, it could have been the work of the
Albinos.

I dried my tears and Tiffany smiled weakly at me. She put
her head on my chest and I hugged her.

"Our cries and protest is interesting fodder for their
troubled minds, its entertainment for them," I offered.

"They got us all fucked up," She sobbed. "These leaders
always sayin' now is the time, when it's pass the time.
Everybody out here sufferin' and don't they know it. We
payin' taxes but can't vote or own a gun to protect ourselves
or our family that's why I have no words for white folks."

"Like IsAnthony says, attention whores get pimped first."

"People of color servin' time in prisons to justify budgets,
keep jobs, and sustain industries...it's a sickening thing to be a
part of.

There are generations upon generations upon generations
upon generations of chains, murders and taxes and these fools
get in front of a camera concerned with the ratings for their

show. I don't know how out parents even agreed to this inequity."

"It's not like they had a choice."

"Oh they had a choice," she said wiping the tears from her eyes and sitting up.

"You are always on white folks. It's not like Hispanics, Asians, and other groups don't have it bad…"

"You're right and those groups have it bad to, ya feel me…"

"Right, right…"

"It's a damn shame that you have to have a camera on white folks to have a sliver of hope that you won't be brutalized. They experts at destroying the legacy of every Black male who made the world look at Black folks differently. They always want attention, they own the industry of making up bullshit… aliens, Sasquatch, Vampires, the Loch Ness monster, ghost…"

"Ghost?"

"Yeah, ghost."

"So you don't believe in ghost?"

"Hell naw, when the ghost of millions of slaves start hauntin' the shit out of white folks, then I'll believe, that's how you know that shit ain't real. They minds just create things for more attention."

"I can see why you are so radical."

"Amber, our existence is radical. From the moment you wake up, death is looking you right in the face. We need to stop asking to be loved, and love ourselves. It's always on with people in skin I'm in and nothing… nothing is ever done about it.

"I tell ya, we got too much love in our hearts. We mad weak for this assimilation stuff. Our plight is just entertainment to them. If they catch these murdering arsonists, they'll call them

Midnight

lunatics, deranged and lone wolves when they know damn well these members of their tribe are sane... You know last night was the first time in five years I actually had a conversation with my mother, and it was a good one."

"Those poor people."

"And that little girl."

"You're not safe nowhere."

"Never have been... "

On the way home we heard the news saying that the fires may have been set by a white primacy group, but I knew that it could have been Albinos covering their feeding. I have been having visions of them and their beach bonfires. Lately, there had been more and more reports of blood drained pets being found, damn Albinos! Holly's church was burned down; she was so emotional that she wouldn't leave the house. I'll stop by and check on her.

Soon as I entered, my mother hugged me really tight. She waved her hand, and the smart wall went dark and music began to play. Over the church drums, everyday mom played Marvin Gaye, Gladys Knight, Alexander Nevermind, and Sam Cooke.

I was starting to like Earth, Wind and Fire, Force MD's, Lisa Lisa, and Cult Jam, Alicia Keys, Prince, New Edition, Janelle Monet, and the Ohio Players. Mom says that yesterday's music was the foundation for today's hit songs and today's music teaches children not to appreciate talent. It's not like the teenage opinion carries a lot of weight.

Mom liked to get lost in rhythms. She liked clean rhythms, because they were undistorted. She always had old album covers lying around. Those covers told a story, they were art. I thought she was doing all of it for my benefit. It was probably another one of those things that I would appreciate later. While she cleaned, I nodded my head to the music as I completed my homework.

My mother always played music and then she would reminisce about how she was present when Jesse Owens showed his ass to Hitler. She told me she was serving popcorn to patrons when Gibson first played Wimbledon. She says that in the House of Representatives, her clap was the loudest when Chisholm first took her seat. She claims that she was the inspiration behind the song *Freedom Highway* and that she was there when *Adventures on the Wheels of Steel* was recorded. My mom was a trip.

I watched my mother as she slowly swayed her five foot seven frame. She was a graceful, unapologetic, brown goddess. She was comfortable in whatever her imperfections may be. Even her voice was something that stayed with you. As I looked at her, my eyes saddened because I saw her differently. Now, I saw loneliness.

My father seemed to gain strength with a woman, as if there was a fusion, some kind of nourishment involved. After the involvements, he rose and delved into the world, into his art, and into his battles. He never seemed lonely, just busy. The memory of his activities into woman gave him energy, it completed him.

My mother was also busy, but as I watched her move and hum around the room, I could tell that she felt empty. My presence, in many ways, had fulfilled her, but it was not the electricity or pleasure she bathed in when my father lied inside of her. The act of taking him, those near-death acts of love, were acts of birth and rebirth, for those moments, my mother bore man. She knew that my father needed peace, and

when he was inside of her, they both had it. I left the house
wondering if I would ever have peace.

I was momentarily frightened by the loud rumbling of
thunder, but I was excited by the lightning that preceded it.
Lightning gave my dull hue a little glow. I was as aware of the
weather as I was of the lookouts on stoops. I didn't want to
get caught in a downpour or caught in some gangland
retribution. I tried to stay above it all.

As a matter of course I went over my studies as I balanced
on beams, held on to planks with the skill of an Olympic
gymnast, and flipped off of construction equipment. I only
stopped my floor routines to put my earpiece back in, to
watch the wind carry my breath, or to watch my silhouette
dance across the walls of buildings. Every night, I went
further.

I roamed the numbered streets and all the streets named
after historical figures. To keep it interesting, one night I
meandered down Chestnut, Walnut, Almond, and all the nut-
represented streets. The next night, I roamed Pine, Oak,
Cedar, Birch, Willow, Chestnut, Elm, Wood, Ash, Maple, and
Myrtle. Next week, maybe I'd do the fruits Lime, Lemon,
Apple, Orange, and Cherry Avenues. I never knew. I did know
that the only time I got to stand tall was in the shadows. I was
not a professional hobo, I was an explorer.

Most of the large buildings in the city were back lit and that
helped conceal me. Buildings where secret meetings were
held were no longer so secret. I made note of the unassuming
homes with two car garages that were really disaster shelters
full of guns, communication equipment, and food. I stayed
away from cemeteries, where they harvest the organs of the
murdered poor and Compton.

MG Hardie

While outside of apartment complexes, I looked through the small windows that revealed the inhumanity of humans. I saw everything, but mostly people having affairs. It is a cold thing when your woman was someone else's side chick.

At two in the morning, the city was a playground, mine. The legal and physical constraints enforced by the day were removed by the night. I frequented buildings where individuals were swallowed up whole and new ideas didn't survive long. My nightly trespasses included museums, large cranes high above the street, construction sites, climbing over fences, and leaping from aircraft hanger to hanger at the regional airport.

It was hard for me to describe, but from twenty nine stories up, nothing really moved when you looked down on it. The view from the mid-level building was where I saw life happening. I saw people crazying on by. I saw them proudly displaying the price tags they didn't even know they had. I saw them running around town going full-ho on people.

The higher I went the more imperfect joining's, unleveled balconies, padlocked doorways, and a host of other safety violations I saw. Those things usually went unnoticed. I had been on roofs and ledges that birds had never been on before. Performing a death defying act for the tenth time wasn't the adrenaline rush you would think it would be. My hacking the tunnels, the hospitals, the power stations, the city was about freedom.

Whites fancy themselves adventurers or explorers, but it was really an unrecognizable sickness that caused them to risk life and limb while a friend filmed their near death extremeness. Black people defied death by mere existence. Even with all their study and preparation these thrill seekers hadn't attempted the feats I had nightly.

Midnight

In the face of uncertain death I climbed twenty stories only to hurl myself across dark chasms just to get from one block to the next. No safety net, no parachute, no camera, no friend, and no backup plan. My existence was all the evidence needed. I didn't need to document it because I'd do it all again the next day, all I left were footprints.

It was amazing how things you repeated in school every day became a part of your life. I found that I looked at advertisements for correct sentence structure; sometime the scientific names of plants and animals randomly pop into my head. Those were the things that filtered through my mind before I made it home.

I arrived just before four a.m. for my two hours of sleep. My mother was in the garden on the side of the house. The only time my mom moved at a consistent human pace was when she was in the garden.

My mom loved being among the Catchflies. She spent a lot of time in the garden with the Wisteria Floribunda and honeysuckles. Four o'clock was when the procurement elders arrived with our blood deliveries. Four o'clock was also when our Moonflowers bloomed. Moonflowers reminded me of myself, dull, lonely, and unremarkable during the day and in full bloom during the night.

My mother's garden was an edible mosaic of tomatoes, sugar snap peas, radishes, and basil. I grabbed the hand pruners and tended to the blue marble and banana trees, I planted those. The others were from the ranks of flowers that did not hate the moon, but quietly yearned for the sun.

I kept Indian hemp plants around mostly for the Grets otos, Glasswing butterflies, another creature that was just as invisible as I was. My mother didn't look up as she prepared the flower bed to receive the Epiphyllum oxypetalum. That was a cactus, but it didn't look like one.

"This is a confusing time for you, but it's a special time," my mother said softly. "You must always be mindful that there are humans who live to hunt us. There are covens that believe the Uhura coven has lost the will to fight, that we are weak. Even with all of that, your biggest fight will come from within."

Just then, a thick fog surrounded our home. The procurement elder had arrived with his usual subtle fanfare, bringing with him a fresh case of blood and just as quickly as the fog rolled in, it was gone.

Some elder's were even said to possess the Hellfire ability, the command of fire. I don't think the elders can speak. Well, I'd never heard one speak. Since they're all telepathic, they don't have much use for things like vocal cords. They could hear your thoughts and you could hear theirs, if they wanted you to.

The elders hardly make a sound, that's an ability I needed. Elders moved so fast, it could hardly be said that you had seen one move at all. My mother came out the house and back into garden and Jill Scott drifted from our house.

"You see, blood is critical for life, but when ingested by humans, it is toxic. In small amount it won't hurt you, but the more they drink of it, the greater the damage will be," she said.

"Are we demons?"

"Demons... even if there were such a thing as a demon, they would have a creator. We are human and inhuman at once. No one wishes to hear what we call ourselves so we are known by many names, nephalem, empusa, vrykolakas, strigoi, upir, vampire, vampire being."

"What about…" I said as I looked through my backpack to pull out a book and showed it to my mother.

"*Dracula,*" chuckled my mom. "That book, humans took information about Cain's early descendants and applied it to us. Dracula was no vampire. Those stories are based on Vlad. Vampire lurked the primeval forests of Mexico long before Cortes thought of coming across the oceans. The Assyrians knew of the vampire before the first brick of their empire was laid. The vampire is feared by the Chinese, by the Indian, and the South American alike. Arabs tell stories of wanderers who haunt lonely crossways attacking and devouring unhappy travelers.

"Blood is the force behind out abilities, it makes them stronger. Blood is the meeting place for God and creation. Humans from China to Arabia to the Romans have acknowledged the significance of bloods.

"*If any man whosever of the House of Israel, and of strangers that sojourn among them, eat blood I will set my face against his soul, and will cut him off from among his people,* Leviticus XVII 10-14."

"Mom, that sounds like bad news for humans who like their food rare," I said, playing with my eyeteeth.

"If they only knew… Ages ago, humans formally discussed and debated Vampirism. We didn't fare well, frankly, because we had become hedonist. The vampire was out, and it was vainglorious. Vampires are the stuff fallen angels are made of.

"The jugular vein runs on both sides of the neck, it is right next to the carotid artery. Another good place is the inner thigh, but that's another subject. Just feeling the warmth of a still beating heart is like nothing you've ever felt. Opening up a jugular vein and just feeding... a hint of rust... salt... spicy... aftertaste..."

"Mom... mom..."

"Yes, I fed on a human once."

"You killed them?"

"Almost. I was young, impulsive, driven by the thirst and little else."

"What stopped you?"

"Your father."

"Dad..."

"That's how we met. The human didn't bleed out, but they were left with no memory of what occurred. I'm not proud of what I did, mind you." My mother picked up her shears, composed herself, and continued speaking. "That moment was the first time the thirst left me. The oxidation, the hemoglobin, the human life force is overpowering. We know that processed, supplements, and synthetics don't work. Blood is rich in iron, the human body absorbs iron faster and in richer quantities than plants do.

"We need blood to survive. The human body creates a lot of things but it has difficulty excreting excess iron. This can cause an iron overdose, a build-up of fluid in the lungs, and nervous disorders. Vampire bodies are equipped to ingest iron, and we need huge amounts to sustain our existence and balance our hormones. The pull we feel is called The Thirst.

Blood Lust is an overwhelming urge to feed on blood; this is something we must never give into. Even though we drink blood almost daily, the thirst is really never quenched."

"Is that why I always feel hungry?"

"Yes. It takes discipline to conquer it. As you've noticed, we don't have cycles like human females, we don't waste blood. Vampires can suck blood from other vampires, but it is primarily during mating. When our teeth enter the body of another vampire, it causes such an aroused state that accelerates the body's survival reaction. Male vampires are very promiscuous, if you can call it that. You have to be a bad bitch to be able to arouse someone who can read your thoughts and drinks blood with morning breakfast.

"During mating, your powers intensify on each other, it make you powerfully naked. The birth process ages us; it takes half of our life force. A vampire without children can live for hundreds of years. This is why we pride ourselves in our children. Your father and I may not see a day over one hundred and twenty five, but you are our pride and joy.

"Adam and Eve were blessed to be fruitful and multiply, Lilith was not, neither was her seed. Once our kind hit puberty, aging slows. The only thing that rapidly ages us is children. Together, we are strong, it is the only way we survive... mwisho." And, with that, my mother ended the lesson.

I think mom felt I may be in danger of losing who I was, so her lessons are always timely. Even in her gardening clothes, you could clearly see that she had it in the all the right places. I still had it in the wrong places. My mother was hit on by young guys all the time and she effortlessly brushed them off. She was so used to attention that it didn't register as an ego stroke.

My mother had an old vampire upbringing where the youth stayed out of grown folks' business and you were thankful for the small things. She didn't believe that playing spades, dominoes, and having a good time damned the already damned to hell. Elders were respected above all, and when you were out of place, you would get disciplined as if you'd lost your ever-loving mind.

My mom used natural products on her customers. She did weaves, but she didn't like to. Every day, she was down at the salon educating sista's on hair and on how to take care of ourselves. She liked to break down barriers to closeness. I liked the way she always mixes in some history. She was by no means, a hard woman to get along with. She told me that she wasn't the kind of woman who would fight for equality in the work place and then again at home.

My mom was full of surprises. She spoke countless languages and not a day went by without her telling me that I was beautiful. She hugged me all the time. She listened to me and she was patient. What more could a daughter ask for? I was impressed watching my mom just being a woman and exerting her power. I entered the house and curled up to sleep.

Tonight once again, the dream got the better of me and I woke up sweaty with the sheets bunched up between my legs. I showered, dressed in something stylishly comfortable, and went to the Tết Festival in Westminster with JD.

The Tết Festival is the celebration for the Vietnamese New Year. It was the most important celebration of Vietnamese culture. The festival celebrates the arrival of spring. There were thousands of people there. I had a blast, even though I didn't understand everything that was being said.

As we walked through the colorful cultural showcase there were bands, violinist, and people dressed in traditional Vietnamese garb. I saw a lot of colorful silk sashes. There was a Miss Vietnam of Southern California contest and it was filled with young, talented, beautiful women, all of whom JD seemed to drool over.

On the way home JD told me that he had been before but now he was fascinated by it all. I was too; it was a cultural

Midnight

rave like the Electric carnival without the drugs. He considered auditioning for the part of Romeo in Angel Beach's production of Shakespeare's Romero and Juliet. I thought he'd make a good Romeo; I agreed to help him read for the part.

Later that night, I restrained my hair, and was eleven stories up listening to music, pondering the meaning of life. Look at these humans tightly clutching their mobile phones, waiting, praying, and hoping that somebody thinks them worthy of being contacted.

They've convinced themselves that what they wear, what they say, how they walk, what do is so unique, so special. I watch them pretend that it's another person's fault they are the way they are. It's strange that they are all offended and all victims...

The festival was a celebration of life; the bright Vietnamese future was on full display. And, I was the one sneaking out at night to raise hell. I was the one living a lie. My future was a matter of life and death; after all you can't fight the night.

Chapter Nine

Out of the shadows, I decided that vampires needed to be in control of our own narrative. I could find a shadow anywhere, even at night, especially in The Bottoms. I had gotten to know all kinds of people. Caucasians aren't all bad; you could say that they have a bad reputation. I mean you can't expect them to just give up their privilege. I wouldn't give up my growing abilities because someone complained about it.

Bad actors come in a variety of shapes, sizes, and races. Take these two wrong-hooders who just entered the party with the intent of shooting it up. There aren't any white people involved with their actions. These Black guys just want to cause maximum damage over a block they don't even own. They don't own any property on the block they claim, but they are out here in these streets ready to miscellaneously put holes in people over it.

I am sure that everyone was happier that I just happened to trip them on my way out. The guns in their waist showed and their scheme was exposed. Before the cops arrived they had the shit beat out of them, but didn't nobody die. There was a good versus bad relationship poor people had with law enforcement, it's complicated, but I had to be more mindful of the brand of human I hung around.

I lived in a country that was a serial abuser of non-white people, even the non-abusers were less than kind to vampire. The law had been a weapon used against black bodies, black bodies like mine. Each of us was one action away from having a curbside memorial. One step away from becoming a hashtag.

Most people don't drive drunk. Most people don't assault people. Most people aren't out here scheming. Most people get up go to work, pay bills, and take care of their children, but even within the good of man I see the struggle with villainy. The struggle is for it not become them.

Black reality was not able to be heard by white people and played up by so-called leaders. The people in The Bottoms never knew what the next day might require of them, so they filled their lives with sighs. They had kids out of anger so they could pour rage into them. It bothered me that I had done nothing to change the attacks by Albinos or any of this.

Every section of the city had its gangsters. It seemed that society wanted, or needed the lower status with low paying jobs, poor schools, and worse teachers. They needed someone to play the foil to their heroism, and they found the group to fulfill that role. Meanwhile, politicians tried to convince the masses that they really wanted the situation to change. If it changed, why would you need them?

With all of that in play, of course, some young guys would do what they could to survive, like drop out of school and further their downward spiral by fathering multiple children with multiple mothers. With no skill and no options, they'd do what they must, even if that meant breaking the very laws that were put in place to ensnare them.

People graduate college thinking that they escaped, that they are smarter, but they still end up paying for those who haven't escaped; I wonder who came up with this endless cycle. I see eager young girls sleeping with guy after guy for money, or worse, for nothing. Some of them only had children so they could qualify for programs and benefits.

Midnight

But, what else do they know? What else have they been taught? What else have they been shown? They hadn't been shown how to work with someone, together. They hadn't been shown how to love. They were forgotten, cast aside and they had become skilled at squeezing a lifetime of bad decisions into one night.

I saw them proudly bouncing their ass and give away their intellectual property. They believed they were descendants of slaves, not the heirs to thrones. To the social order, their disrespect was profitable. Every act of lawlessness, every teenage indiscretion showed the powerful of how successful they had been at creating the illusions. The rules were put in place not to profit from success, but from struggles.

The Bottoms were like a concentration camp, where abuses happened and you get away with it. It was hella cutty there even the big crime bosses don't live near it. The Bottoms is where most of the police went for habitual and repeat offenders. Some places turned hood after dark, but not The Bottoms. The Bottoms was hood all the time.

We define people by putting them into any box that's convenient for us to understand. Adrian said that slights of economic prudence are just easier to understand as racism and I beginning to sound like him. It took me all night to find some inspiration.

In school, guys had been put on notice; those that did not listen got treated like any other acquaintance. I still received a number of roses from guys that I knew and those that I didn't. It was just my luck that Valentine's Day fell on a blood moon. Adrian and I hadn't talked about that day, we didn't even mention it. I assumed I was going to get nothing. When I got home on the porch, there was a bouquet of multi-colored roses. They were from Adrian. The simple *Happy Valentine's Day!* on the card made me weak.

I put on a saucy single shoulder red dress, he swooped me up on the scooter, and we went to Shoreline for dinner. We spent the evening holding hands and listening to music while walking along the boardwalk. We sat on the rocks and listened to the waves push up against them. There was always so much I had to say to him, but when we were alone I never knew where to begin.

The way he looked into my eyes, the way his hand slowly moved from my knee to my thigh, forced me to keep quiet. I'll admit it; I was in love with him. Right then and there, I should have kissed him. I wanted to kiss him under a sky filled with a thousand stars, but the blood moon rendered me speechless. I should have told him how I felt, but I could only rest my head on his shoulder and exhale. The blood moon had me off balance, I didn't know what would have happened if I had acted on how I felt.

I put my arms around him and buried my face into his warm back, and he drove me home. My dress flapped as the wind rifled through my hair and I sat on the back of his scooter. He gave me a single blue rose, bluer than anything I had ever seen, and we said our goodbyes. He smiled at me and I watched his scooter turn the corner.

It was one of those rare nights where the wind howled and you could hear dead leaves slowly scrape across the concrete. I went to the side of my house and put my rose neatly in the garden. I exhaled, put on my gloves, and climbed on top of my house. I gathered myself, leapt onto the next house, and ran.

My name is Amber. I am vampire and my night has just begun.

Midnight

From my perch, I watched the police go into communities trying to get people to say and do things they wouldn't normally say and do. They even broke the law to get a person to break the law. They posed as bad guys to get people who barely survived the opportunity to break the law. From my point of view, bad guys didn't need extra motivation to be bad guys.

The sound of the ghetto bird drowned out the sound of my music, the bulk of my allowance was spent on lost headphones. Every other street light in The Bottoms didn't work; after all, the lighting was less for the safety of residents and more for law enforcement visibility. Most of Angel Beach basked in sodium vapor light. The more affluent areas had switched to the brighter LED lights and I had to be more cautious there.

In The Bottoms, you could get murdered over shoes, headphones, or a look, as off-leash dogs wandered side streets. More people were in project housing here than anywhere else in the city. The people didn't have enough income to move out, so they had to live in a building where one floor was a drug lab, and the other floors were full of screaming women and children.

Everyone stayed high so that they didn't have to look at the same four dirty walls; they stayed drunk so they could go to the same crummy job day in and day out. I saw them watch mindless show after mindless show so their thoughts from don't focus on the mess that is their existence. The ones that stayed strapped had the most problems, the biggest being accuracy.

There were more vile things going on in better neighborhoods, but The Bottoms was the only Angel Beach area colored red in every app I've seen. The smells drifting up from the street hardly reached beyond the fifth floor. There isn't a building over five stories in The Bottoms. After all, it was the projects. It smelled of gun powder, body fluids, and old blood. It wasn't safe for anyone to walk around there alone; it wasn't even safe when you weren't alone.

I was rooftop running as usual when I heard the sound of crashing trashcans. I heard breaking glass, shouts, and muffled sounds. I looked over the ledge and there was Rick in an alley being overpowered by five guys. He must have been on his way home. You could tell that his attackers were skilled at putting their foot into the asses of other people.

Rick got in a few hits of his own until a bottle broke over his head. He stumbled into the middle of the alley. One attacker cursed at him as another punched him the face. Once he was on the ground, they kicked him in various parts of his body as he moaned. They took turns hitting him. Finally, they lifted him up and held him up against the wall. One goon grabbed his face, and said "You will respect us." Then a ghoul punched him hard in the stomach.

Unable to take the brutality, I descended the building like lightening. I landed on two thugs and slid into the body of another. I followed that up with a cross knife kick to his face. My red, single shoulder dress flowed around me as I spun counter clockwise and landed two precise kicks to the left and right jaw before the main goon could lift his weapon and fire, unconsciousness was immediate.

I floated through the air and landed another series of blows and down went another. I ducked and connected with an uppercut, and another one was on his back. I ran off of a wall and landed a precise butterfly kick. As the last thug lost consciousness, I dropped to my knees and slowly fell to my

Midnight

back. The last thing I saw was a bruised Rick kneeling over me.

The clank of cheap china prompted me to open my eyes. The apartment was small; it was bare bones except for the large, digital wall monitor that randomly displayed gorgeous photo after gorgeous photo. The photos were so visually distracting that I started to rethink the flicks I took and erased in the bathroom. I didn't know Rick had that kind of talent.

The photos were perfect, the tones, the light, the textures, the movements, and the possibilities down to the smallest detail. Images of a man playing golf in the rain, a boy with a ball, a couple having sex, and a woman's eye filled with tears.

The photos were like a song strung together. It was his vision of a perfectly captured world and each picture told a different story. His soft eye brought life to tides, sunsets, and smiles. The images were how he processed the world. He took a hold of life one picture at a time, crowds of people, shooting stars, constellations, but not one picture of himself. He caught me looking at his old glass lens camera photos.

"You 'ight?

"I think so. Nice little place you've got here," I said sarcastically while sitting up on the tattered couch.

"It's mine," he shot back from the kitchen.

"So, this is yo' spot..."

"Yeap."

"Well, ALYAH."

"Huh?"

"A... L... Y... A... H..."

"What?"

"At Least You Ain't Homeless."

"True dat."

"Awwww…" I said as I noticed the scrapes on my leg and my damaged music player. I must have fainted and I still had to make it home. Right now, I was a mess. I didn't even know where I was, and Rick walked towards me.

"What kind of basketball moves were those? For months, I have watched you stumble around school. And here you are spending your nights swinging around poles in a dress and heels, kicking people in the face, making it rain."

"I was not making it rain. I practice martial arts in my free time," I sighed, standing up.

"Uumm hmmm, in alleys… at night, and you expect me to believe that?"

"Not everyone is afraid of the dark, some people embrace it."

Without warning, he tried to slap me. I avoided his attempt, grabbed his arm, and put him in a goose neck wrist lock, a very uncomfortable position.

"Ow… ow… owww…. I was just testing you. I notice everything, even those rather sharp teeth of yours."

"You saw them?" I asked, covering my mouth as I let him go. Weak, I leaned against the wall.

"How could I miss them?" Rick said, brushing himself off and turning on songs by the artist Rome. "Don't you live in a castle, a cave, or something?"

"Ha… ha… very funny… Perhaps I have a torture chamber… Rick, you know where I live."

"I thought I did," he said, walking into the kitchen as I continued to look around his apartment. "I spent the morning trying to get my head wrapped around this whole thing. I thought vampires were just Hollywood bullshit. Not for a moment did I believe vampires actually existed. So that's why you and your friends like to wear black?"

"They're not like me…"

"Right. You know Adrian is a Christian, right?"

"Yes."

"…and, my best friend." I wrinkled up my face at Rick. "Just checking," he said, handing me hot hibiscus tea.

"This is awkward."

"Who you telling?" As I moved to leave, he stepped in front of me with his hand out.

"Whoa… whoa… there is no need to be nervous," he said, moving the cold pack on his jaw to his ribs. "If that's how you want to spend your nights, then that's how you spend them. I bet you see all kinds of things, have you watched me before?"

"Ain't nobody stalkin' you, I watch everyone," I said. "Go ahead and ask."

"Ask what?" he said.

I knew the question that had been on the tip of his tongue ever since I woke up on his couch.

"So, do you go around biting people?' he blurted out as he shifted through the broken pieces of his camera on his counter top.

"I don't do that. I really have no idea what I am doing."

"Who does?"

"Are you going to tell him?"

"Tell him what?'

"Are you going to tell anyone?"

"Not my place."

"I guess I owe you an explanation…"

"You don't owe me nuthin'. You could have easily just stood by, but you didn't. You saved my life, to me that counts for everything. As for those retractable teeth, I didn't see anything. For a little girl who doesn't like attention, this kind of stuff can put you on the radar real fast. You might want to consider wearing a mask. I mean, running on walls, a cheat 1080, the glowing eyes, and the growls… incredible."

"A cheat 1080? Ummm, I'm sorry about that."

"Don't be, lead with that next time."

"Everything happened so fast. I don't know what came over me." My eyes filled with tears.

"Whatever it was, I am glad it did." He put his arms around me. "It was hot!" he said, wiping away my tears.

"Who were those guys?"

"Just some guys."

"I was just trying to scare them."

"They needed to get that work though…"

"Yeah they did."

"I almost didn't believe what I saw, so I know they didn't."

"You fight pretty well, too."

"Not well enough," he said, rubbing his jaw.

"Fighting them, saving you actually felt kind of good. You know, if you are being harassed, you can always go to the police."

"Teachers, nurses, lawyers, doctors, and the police have to be sold that you are worthy of being helped. Amber, you are a straight badass," he said with an almost giddy tone to his voice.

"Yeah, wait until you see me kick ass in a jean jacket." I chuckled.

"I am making crunchy berry filled breakfast sandwiches, or do you need something more exotic?" he said, looking up. He pressed down into the hot cookware with a spatula in his right hand and turned a page of his history book with the other.

"Ummm, yeah, I really have to go." I finished my tea and headed to the door.

Midnight

"See ya at school," he uttered as I walked out the door.

Rick lived on a street filled with condemned buildings and turned over trash bins. The streets were so unsafe that children had no idea what hopscotch was. Children didn't play hide and seek or red light-green light. I was not even sure they would know what those games were. The sun was hours from touching anything, but outside of the apartment near the discarded chairs and furniture, toddlers were already playing in their diapers and underwear.

I rode the earliest bus I could home. I sat uncomfortably in that sparely lit bus looking like illicit sex and a bad hangover. My asymmetrical, sleeveless dress had seen better days. If I had more blood, I wouldn't have passed out. I knew sooner or later the streets would tell on me. In one night, I had become both fact and fiction. In one night I had become the most frightening thing in The Bottoms. I made it home an hour before sunrise.

"Oh, so you are just going to start acting human now, huh? Lawd, give me strength!" my mother sternly said as I hurried to my room.

Chapter Ten

The heat, combined with cool water from the Pacific Ocean, created deep blankets of fog that extended deep within Angel Beach. The evaporated moisture was why so many of my mornings and nights were fog laden. The fog obscured even the tallest building from view, so it had no problem hiding me. From my perches near the beach, I could see the mist settle at the foot of every structure.

The fog rolled in fast and only got thicker. It became so thick that when I was on the beach at two in the morning, I couldn't see the docks. The first time I heard the foghorn, it was so loud that it startled me. As the fog moved towards the shore, the signal blared a warning to all passing ships. The school year was halfway over and the horns were hardly noticeable, but tonight they were especially loud and constant.

Maybe what I felt about Adrian wasn't natural. Maybe my nerves the first day of school caused me to amplify emotions onto Adrian without even knowing it. I was happy to have that first day feeling for a day, a week, and now it's been months, but was it me? The questions were clearly my mind's attempt to massage the last remaining remnant of any insecurity I had left. There were a dozen of girls after him, so what did he see in me?

The foghorn sounded again and snapped me out of my thoughts as I made my way along the rocks. In the darkness, crabs and stingrays followed me as I meandered along wet rocks... I always have treats for them. I was headed toward the aqueducts and the homeless encampments.

MG Hardie

The mist had been good to me; it allowed me to remain invisible. I spent a lot of time not being noticed. The fact was that I'd never be human and now I didn't know if I wanted to be. I hung out on the top of hospitals and old folks homes. I watched humans be born and I watched them die. I watched them get shot in the middle of the street for no good reason. Humans were so angry in life, but so peaceful in death.

You'd be surprised how many people lived in the storm drains of various towns. These homeless camps were typically close to the towns that threw away the most food. A city's fingerprints lied in its streets and alleyways. I saw my reflection as I zipped-lined from buildings to building. I am invisible, but with the hoodie on, I am unrecognizable to myself. From atop ferris wheels, bridges, and high voltage wires, I could barely see the pavement below me through the fog.

I didn't sit around thinking; my thoughts were active, bass lines replaced loneliness. I had the vocals of Aubrey Graham, Kimberly Jones, O'Shea Jackson, and Jermaine Lamarr Cole to keep me company. During my explorations, I had fallen in love with music. I fell in love with the rhythm of it, the mathematics of it and the sheer power of it. Through music, I had become quite good at expressing myself.

My flow was simple and my poetic rhymes were complex. When I graduated to triple entendres in my storytelling, I put my poetically articulated words to music. With rooftops as my stage, I lyrically cut loose. My poems were fluid, dexterous and unpredictable. I was pulling off long-form narratives filled with wit, symbolism, metaphors, and imagery.

Over instrumental beats, I performed from one rooftop venue to the next. When my dreams weren't blood filled, I was on stage in front of shouting masses while my words rode on the sickest of beats. Dreams of rocking a mic were impossibilities; there was no audience for my poems except cats, possums, and the stars. For me, there would be no likes, comments, or promotional campaigns. Putting me on stage would give the world the boogeywoman their minds thirsted for. Being a vampire was like being a rock star, only no one knows it.

The only person I revealed my rhymes to was Tiffany. Now she thinks that I am the realest around, so that makes two of us. I walked and all that I was walked with me. I ran and everything I was ran with me. The same was true about my lyrical skills, but there was absolutely no chance that I could rep the west.

Adrian's crew and mine didn't always hang out together. We had been sending each other instaflicks and vidstrips of what we were doing and eventually our groups got together. The groups were often together, but we still looked for opportunities to be team us.

My nose became increasingly sensitive. The air quality in Angel Beach varied drastically depending on where you were. The West Side had the worst because of the oil refineries; there was an air quality alert every other day. Mornings of burning throats lend themselves to large numbers of children with headaches, asthma, and other respiratory conditions.

It was not exactly the Inglewood oil fields, which were surrounded by a million people, but the nitrogen dioxide was noticeable to me. Those types of adverse conditions don't develop in vampires unless the blood sources became tainted. Naples and Belmont Shore had relatively clean air. Affluent residents would never allow oil refineries or fracking around their children, and their land wasn't cheap, either.

Grease and food smells seeped from the bins that sought to contain them and filled the night air, but we still had a blast. It was my suggestion that we go from shop to shop instead of sitting in eateries. I had to because I could smell the garlic on everyone's food.

I could really feel my body growing in places where I least expected. I was two inches taller and up a bra size. I could feel my ass pressing against the inside of my pants and my hips were really working my stretch jeans. I could no longer wear my little girl dresses; I knew that I had to donate them. I wasn't a little girl long enough.

Having people interested in me because of the way I looked was a new level of being uncomfortable. From the looks I had, it was obvious that other people noticed my body changes. Guys wanted me to believe that a subtle smile and sad eyes was their type. I knew it wasn't; only a fool would believe that garbage. Those guys only read the headlines.

Every day, I heard little boys with thick eyebrows talk about how they would merk that or how they would be the best I ever had. They hooted and howled like untrained pets, like I was some basic girl. When they got shown up, they retaliated with feeble complaints of how girls had too many don'ts, and stops, and not enough don't stops. They need to stick to the boy on boy thoughts in their head.

Unfortunately, and depending on what you were wearing, some people stared at you like you were a stripper about to provocatively take off all of your clothes. I usually got guys to keep on walking with the Bounce Glare. It didn't happen often but there were always a few guys the glare didn't work on.

Today was one of those days in which the glare didn't work because some random guy in one of the school's smaller hallways had the nerve to come up and smack me hard on my ass. I dropped my books, and quickly dented a green and gold locker with his back before the smile of accomplishment left his face. "Not these cakes!" was the only thing I said before letting him go.

The fear in his eyes allowed me to see into his mind. He was just another little boy who would remember his sexual partners as trophies, to every now and then be dusted off, reminisced over, and put back. He would soon be a man who would wake up lonely one day, wondering why his sex game was never enough to keep a woman. I quickly picked up my books and headed to the principal's office. That was the first time my ass had been touched by someone other than me. I said I didn't like it, but I did.

Everyone's body has a certain combination to it, and Adrian seemed to know mine. At the most random moments I could feel his breath on my skin. I could feel him touching me. I imagined myself taking him, tasting him...Things were getting out of hand; the heavens were out of order. Something had to be done, so I ignored him... delete... delete... delete.

I tried to avoid his cute little looks. I turned the hallways into mazes. I didn't so eagerly sit by him in Chemistry. I did what I could to not to be available to him. Not seeing him didn't mean I couldn't still feel him. The more I tried to forget the feelings, the more I thought about them. Adrian began asking Holly and Tiffany what was wrong with me.

Today, I had on a little make-up. Whenever I used make-up, I used very little because my face was well defined, what I had on was enough for anyone to notice the change. In the hallway, I saw Adrian turn the corner and enter the hallway, my heart pounded. His eyes rose and so did the hairs on the back of my neck. He looked at me and I felt weak. I darted into the nearest bathroom and threw some water on my face. As steam from the faucet rose, I looked into the mirror.

I was losing it. There were wrecking balls in my brain, a ghost town in my heart, and the whispers grew louder. I couldn't fight it all. I was, for the sake of everyone, fully prepared to move seats, change classrooms, and give him up. He had me, but I was willing to give him up. It was as if my efforts against losing myself only served to pull me in deeper.

My plan was to stay in the bathroom until he passed by. Well, that was the plan before I noticed the urinals. I was in the boy's bathroom. Two boys approached me. I turned off the water and gave them the meanest glare in my arsenal, and said, "Don't even think about it!" Only, I didn't actually say the words. I thought I did, but my mouth never opened. The boys stopped in their tracks, looked confused, took another glance at my cakes, and quickly exited the bathroom.

The strangeness of me being in the boy's bathroom was confusing enough; it was quick, so I don't think they were sure if I actually said something or not. I was quite sure that I hadn't said anything. I was quite sure that I projected it.

Trying to avoid Adrian only made my days longer and my nights colder. It had the opposite effect and he became the only person I was nervous around. I am in Adrian withdrawal. Last month, I couldn't get the thoughts of kissing him out of my head and now we aren't even talking. It had been the longest two weeks of my life.

He gave me my space and it tore me apart, even his playful looks had me losing my damn mind. He was tall, cute, and his skin tone was lighter than mine, so girls hated on me for no other reason than my presence in the middle of the brown color spectrum.

Midnight

There were plenty of people whose lives were so inert that they would happily hate on you. I could complain about people who talked in negative ways about me, but why? You will be talked about even if you did everything right, so why complain?

As nearest I could tell, all humans were addicted to something, drugs, food, and sex. They were addicted to sensations. Humans were sick, dark, passionate, and violent. Humans are the worst opportunist and most of it made no sense at all as I walked to school against the relentless sun. Yes, I drink blood, but it is the human mistreatment of people that's monstrous. They were the real monsters, not me.

Humans say to themselves that they don't want to be a statistic, when they were the statistic. Of course, I listened to them when they called themselves princess or queen. I used to think that when some girl you hardly knew asked if you were going to this event or to that party, she was trying to be your friend.

They would talk to me about the party like it was the shit because we were going. Those girls smiled in your face, but when you got to the party the jealousy was thick. At the gatherings, guys thought that wearing a dress was the first move, and sometimes it was. Everything was about perception and perception is whatever you were told it is.

The boys fight and bust caps at each other, but the girls, the girls were the ones who needed to be taken to task. They were fighting, robbing, drugging, sexing, and cutting their wrist, and a year later, they would bring another life into the world. We were kids, we did amazing things, but really none of us knew anything.

Unsupervised kids got involved in all types of things. If you let bored kids be around other bored kids, that was like asking for trouble. The skirt wearing girls I attended parties with only wanted me there when they kissed boys and leaned back into the couch. And, just like that, I became the independent witness to their sexual forays, a cosigner. They were always *too* on. They were the kind of chicks that show up unannounced, actin' crazy, and refuse to leave; that was not how royals acted.

At these parties, it usually goes down like this. You are marginally enjoying yourself sitting in a dim room listening to loud music, when one of the girls you came with gives you her drink and asks you to watch it for her. You do, and the next thing you know, the bitch is on her knees in front of some dude and everyone is looking at you.

The expression on my face was like, 'I hardly know this bitch.' Everyone tries to get their hooks into someone else, searching for connections. They got me a couple of times with an offer of friendship under false pretense. Telling everyone we are friends, but we ain't really friends.

I find random sexual interactions to be ridiculous. Not ridiculous because of the acts, ridiculous because of the proper way humans liked to carry themselves. They seem so above the act until something primal is turned on; when nature hits them they forgot all formalities and pretense. Instincts cause them to behave in ways they would never otherwise. I behave this way too which makes it even more ridiculous.

I was not completely innocent in all of this I babysat a couple of drinks and passed a few blunts, but I was not trying to be anywhere where I am not in control. Those girls I came with undressed quickly because their minds were already naked and the guys, well, they never stood a chance. Having a witness made it easier for them to go beyond all the way.

Midnight

The other new skirt wearing thugette you came with was already on her seventh shot and performing nasty tricks on the floor. When both girls reached out and squeezed my thigh, I was like *what tha hell*. Their actions were designed to get me on my back, on my knees or both. I was not going to be the one walking home without so much as a towel to wash up with….just mistreating her mocha caramel skin.

Kids were familiar with the fashionable substances because we gave them nicknames and popular songs are made about using them. Only a few kids went to extremes with drugs, but all of us had smoked, injected, jello-shotted, snorted, dripped, or wrapped it in a plastic bag. When you're our age, there's plenty of contagious dumb shit just lying around for you to pick up.

All of the sexual fumbling around was unnerving to watch and sickening to be a part of, but there was a part of me that wanted to know how it felt. The girls I came with had hoped their performances would urge me to return the favor. I would not. I'm not doing it. I wished I could blame all the nonsense on the perpetrators. However, my anger at these girls allowed me to enter their minds. These two girls were abused, they abused themselves, and they would pass abuse on to others.

One girl's trauma was so vivid that her screaming voice echoed inside my head all night. All females are equally valuable; even if they don't have the body of an ass poppin' video vixen. Some are just terribly misguided. If they'll pretend to be pregnant, you couldn't put anything pass them. Spending your existence wanting to be someone's black china and looking forward to baby showers is no way to live. The way any of it made sense was that they needed the drama; something inside of them wanted it.

MG Hardie

Truthfully, I don't even know why I hung out with those girls in the first place. That was not true, I did know. I did it because I wanted to believe they were drunk enough to think my yellow irises were just the latest contact lenses. I wanted to believe that they were faded enough to not care if I drunk a little blood every now and then. The risk to all vampires was far too great for me to indulge in my growing narcissism; I was not the only Wharton.

Being a vampire was a dilemma of metaphysical proportions before I even knew what being a girl was. I was all for having a good time, but for a girl, everywhere you went there were people who didn't have a problem eating something. Even the ones that found it disgusting still found enough curiosity to try it once or five times. Of course, when they get older, they would unapologetically say, 'One time I...'

Because law enforcement disregards the rights of Black males and because they incarcerate and wantonly kill Black males... At these gathering, I saw many males trapped in female bodies... many of them are pretending more that I am.

'You can't get pregnant from spit,' my lesbian homegirl liked to tell me. You can't, but I could have both on this side of the fence. I'm just saying... So tonight, at this function, I sat there and listened to another kid slightly elongate every profane word. I can't believe that I interacted with the beings that have shorter attention spans than goldfish. These beings ran in packs and popped gum to hide their medicated breath. Their minds and sexuality was not neatly tied together with a pretty bow.

The girls racked up dates, but for them happiness came from consumption. Humans spent their weekends lying awake at night with tears in their eyes believing that they, in spite of themselves, were more than their mistakes. Here nothing was entirely non-consensual and the next day a million guys will nervously wait to see if their partner in the act would blame them for all of it.

"You feeling me?" some random guy that was too close to me said.

"The only thing I am feeling is this music," I responded. *Oh, God, and here comes another one.* I'm getting pretty good at using my powers to make some guy soil himself or throw up on the next dude. They are my anti-thirst powers. Let's see how they like that.

At these gatherings there is no hand holding, just alcohol swallowing, music playing, and ass rubbing, unzipped zippers, and pulled up skirts. When I got invited to parties, it was by guys who wanted to hook up with me. I was not looking for a hook up; I was just looking for fun.

Maybe it was dishonest of me to accept the invitations since I knew what these hand-jerkers wanted. Besides, I never stay long because pushing through crowded, liquored-up living rooms filled with raging hormones and bad attitudes was not my idea of fun.

I wasn't thrilled about going to parties because I was not the best dancer in the world, in the city, or in my own home. When my song came on, I usually put both my hands up and hover by the nearest the wall. That was my move. Holly taught me that if a salesperson was willing to negotiate on the price, you could get it cheaper elsewhere. She is also teaching me how to dance in exchange for salon techniques. She is down five pounds since I got her to stop eating family size potato chips. Overall, she was very, very patient when I stepped on her toes. I loved her.

At the gatherings, mentally, I was as lost as I was on any rooftop in the city. I left the gatherings always needing to clear my head, and every night I found myself high above those places where flawed people were incarcerated to keep jobs, places where the best nurses spent hours drinking, places where most murderers weren't arrested. In those places, entertainers secretly floating rumors about their sexuality, rumors they never confirmed publically, which was a confirmation for those who mattered.

I was vampire before ever being acquainted with beings that alter themselves after looking at a magazine. I was vampire before I knew a girl who paid top dollar to bind her feet. I had the thirst long before seeing a girl wait for a real or imagined slight before fighting tooth and nail over all the unimportant things in a male. I was vampire before I was woman and I was women long before I was Black. My mind was anything but fifteen.

I may have been fifteen, but I know a few things. Simple things such as if you were talking shit on social networks all day, you weren't making millions of dollars, and that getting used was what some people do best. People don't think of the impact a simple thing like where you sat in class can have on your life, I did. The one thing I know for sure is that only cowards sub-hate.

People were always quick to question someone's reason and science, but never their own. When you mixed that in with the incorrect generalizations about males, females, and kids you see humans for what they are, tired organisms hurling greetings of fake sincerity at each other. It had to be some kind of sickness. Better minds than mine have tried to figure all of this out, but were unsuccessful.

The cure for every condition was probably locked away in an uneducated mind somewhere. The darkness was growing thicker and blood was becoming my only comfort. Drinking blood bought me time, gave me power, and it made me feel better, a lot better. And, though I had tried plenty of times, I hadn't been able to project again.

On the weekends, the city was alive with activity, construction, new park dedications, concerts, and fairs. Friday nights were mandatory for teens to dress overly cute before going out. Their flashy outfits clashed with blaring music genres emanating from the vehicles slowly cruising 2nd Street.

Kids behave completely different outside of school. Downtown on weekend nights were filled with hordes of shirtless boys, freestyle dancers, mid-rifted girls, tourists, and groups of teenage Jesus super freaks that chased girls in-between talking about scripture. Souped-up cars bounced by blasting music while kids screaming with their heads out of the window. There were adults out as well, but clearly, kids ran the beach.

Every weekend, up and down Coconut, Almond Avenues, and Angel Beach Boulevard, kids from the city's six high schools intermingled with those who apparently had just finished getting their drink on. People came to the shoreline from all over; they came down Atlantic Avenue from Compton, from Cerritos by way of Carson Street, and from Seal Beach by traveling PCH.

My group went from east to west, from shopping center to strip mall. We often ended up in a movie theater, with everyone stuffing their faces with snacks. There was no surplus of silliness, picture taking, or laughing. Of course, there were a few white girls trying to be down and wanting to stick their nose into some business that wasn't theirs, but we chilled with them too.

The end of winter had proved to be quite cold, but that was when the unspoken competition between females was at its fiercest. Girls used their psychical attributes in the same way boys did in sports; it just looked different when we do it. Boys walk around with no shirts, muscles shirts, and basketball shorts. It was the same as girls wearing cleavage revealing blouses, midriff showing tops, or a mini skirts.

Boys get attention for shots, dunks, leaps, and catches. Girls get attention for walks, struts, bounces, and touches. Boys don't get labeled slut or ho, even the athletic whores. Boys did a lot of loud, obvious things while we girls were often more subtle; hey, being subtle requires a lot of talent. This cannot be understated, we have Park and Rec leagues all the way up to the professionals, and competition is fierce.

Any weather shift gave us a reason to change up our style of attire, so when it's cold you see more pants and coats. But some girls, no matter how cold it was, just had to be seen strutting in shorts and miniskirts. Basketball practice, combined with all the climbing I did at night, really toned my body, so my little shorts were turning some heads. It could be the competition that made me say that, but on Friday's I wore shorts for no other reason than I was surprisingly warm.

There were always more teenagers out on warm nights. I looked amazing in those black, cheetah-skin bootie shoes. Unfortunately, warm nights also brought out ugly toes. I was out every night, but the weekend nights were the only times I could cut loose with friends and not be thought of as strange. My friends wondered where I got the energy, not how I keep beating them in billiards.

Most Fridays, we went out to have a good time, but lately, our group was getting stopped by the police, stopped sometimes twice in the same night. I was frisked by Sergeant Egum. Usually, our group sat curbside, in-between three police cars while flashlight-wielding officers asked us questions, such as where we lived, where we were going, and why we were in the area. Their questions were an effective message that we didn't belong. According to Adrian these police practices were not for anyone's prevention, they were a tool to get young minorities used to being harassed by law enforcement.

"These are the incidents that engineered poverty provides," Adrian said. "Poverty is engineered so that members of the poor become the group that the public doesn't mind taking actions against. Instead of unbought and unbossed the authorities had for sale signs.

"Think about it, all these protests and not one law, not one policy has changed… because these laws and policies are doing what they were designed to do, which is to deliver dark faces into an industry that sustains the country. No law can force respect and the police are often an unjustifiable force that is used on young people. Fighting for citizenship is one thing, fighting for your humanity is another." Adrian was always the quietest when we get stopped, but he was the most affected by theses stops.

I must have been slow or something because I didn't make the connection between the police stops and my skin color. I thought the police were just doing their job. I thought they randomly stopped everyone. As time went on, I saw how they focused on minority groups. Adrian had me thinking about all kinds of things.

The smooth cadence with which Blacks, Latinos, and Asians moved must be a cause for suspicion. Even the officer's shoulder camera did nothing to change their behavior. Perhaps, they were drawn to our youth. Maybe it was the size of our group. Regardless of what it was, somehow we had been labeled universally suspicious

MG Hardie

Tiffany said that our complexion lacked consideration. Each deadly incident with law enforcement brought protests, hashtags, sign holding, and a lot of singing. I saw people rally in the streets and run against the storm with impotent rage. The law was for your body, not everybody.

I could take action, I could do something, but that could make matters worse or better. If I did anything other than being marginally irritated, it could lead to further complications. The police stops did what they were designed to do and that was to put a damper on our weekend activities.

"What is it this time... walking while Black? Breathing while Black? Living while Black!" Tiffany never cooperated. "Loitering... If we are loitering, then everyone here is loitering. Why aren't you stopping them over there? Stop them right there! This shit ain't right and y'all know it. Nothing is wrong until it happens to whites," she'd barked at them.

"Fuck the police!" people across the street yelled.

When Tiffany was on a roll, she talked more shit than a middleweight champ did in their prime. People in our group complained because her remarks often prompted a call to get a female officer to the scene so they could search for drugs. The process was time consuming. Tiff was a mess, but she was right.

The police stops were the main reason we visited different places each Friday. We went from the shore, to downtown, to the town Center, to the go-kart tracks, to the BMX show. We never chilled at the same place two Fridays in a row. The police incidents and Adrian's views on the world gave me more things to meditate on nightly.

Adrian wasn't a genius, but he was intelligent. People think he is uber-serious, but he has a dry sense of humor that didn't immediately show. He and I often used each other as sounding boards for ideas. Now that my period of ignoring him was over, we talked about everything. There was no pressure to have sex and we didn't want each other for our bodies. Well, that was not entirely true. We did play the accidently brush against each other game. The new game made me blush.

Lately, we had been finishing each other's sentences. He wasn't so straight-laced that he couldn't cut loose every now and then. He was not a bad boy, but he was just as fun and a whole lot safer. His body was cut; you could tell by the way his pants hugged his body. Some of these thirsty chicks would do anything to get a hold of his abs. He could take advantage if he wanted to, but he didn't. I got sweated by guys, too, but their blood scent wasn't as balanced as Adrian's.

I was softer than humans. I usually get complimented on how perfectly white my teeth were or how soft my hands were, and I explained that I washed a lot of dishes. There was a pull on me whenever I glanced into his eyes. When we weren't going out in groups, he made simple things like chasing down food trucks and going to the bookstore fun.

I returned home at four a.m., I was afraid to close my eyes, but my body was sore from the night's activities. Sleep came fast, the dream came quick, and the sunrise dawdled.

Chapter Eleven

This close to school, the streets were full of life in the day time. On schools days, the streets are clogged with disordered amounts of construction signs. There are always older men and sometimes women ogling at children as they went to school. I always thought they were looking at me funny, but now I realized that was just how they looked. I mean, I did have on the tightest shorts I had ever worn, but they weren't the tightest of the day.

I retrieved my shades from my single shoulder backpack while a pop song blared from a passing car. Winter had just ended so it was very warm and there was an endless supply of hairy legs and flared-out dresses. When teenagers got together, it didn't take much for neighborhood affiliations to show. The heat seemed to agitate everyone. I heard a lot of slender guys talking tough and threat making, everybody wanted to be ahead of the curve.

Maybe it was the threats I overheard on the way to school that put me in my current state. When I rounded the corner, they were laughing at her. They spoke to her as if they controlled her. I couldn't remember her name, even though I had spoken to her once or twice before. She was nice. Her skin tone was seen by many as vanity.

She wasn't one of those biracial girls who always talked about how good her skin and hair was. She wasn't one of those girls who would always low-key flirt with your man. She wasn't always running around extolling the virtues of being mix raced, as if they created themselves... naw. She quietly did her schoolwork and minded her own business.

Who were those girls to tell anyone that they were not black enough, that they acted white? The girl was envied by those darker than her because of her lighter skin tone. Her white friends make fun of her for the same exact reason. Most people loved her because of her whiteness they also hated her because of it.

I see desperate, frustrated, big eyed girls like her every day. Some so desperate they went beyond the mutilation, past the substances, and straight to wrist slitting just to show them all—like that will teach 'em. They minds so mangled that they believe alcohol, sex, self-defacement and violence was the missing piece to the puzzle of life.

Children wanted to be loved. They wanted to be accepted, to be cool. They didn't want to spend parts of each day crying in a defaced, piss smelling bathroom stall. Children just wanted to finish one thing in their life, even if that one thing was just school. Kids didn't care about priorities, time, or politics. To them, albums sales, how high you jumped, and yards gained trumped police charges, and popularity outweighed social common sense.

As the school year rolled along, the stories of any child's life seemed to get progressively worse. They went to school because it was the law, but the law didn't say they had to eat a meal before attending. The rumbling sounds of their belly often drowned out the noise from their imagination. For many kids, being hungry was a normal state of being. It was a state I knew all too well.

The girl's vaping in the bathroom pissed me off. They weren't being discreet about it; it pissed me off even though that was how you were supposed to do it. The brown nosing girl in third period agitated me. I was agitated by the guy wearing the gray corduroy jacket with brown sneakers. The usual whispers of recent mercy dates agitated me. Maybe I was just unnerved by the lingering affected of the blood moon, my perpetual unclear relationship status, or the looming state benchmark exams.

The right outfit spoke volumes and the outfit I had on just wasn't working for me. It should have said 'leave me the hell alone', but it didn't. I felt constricted. I feel like I have outgrown all of this. If I had stayed under my sheet for another ten minutes, I wouldn't be thinking of derogatory words to use the next semester, I would be focusing on this Chemistry test.

The same guys that had been set tripping with each other all semester were going hard at it. Two fights broke out during first period. Alarms sounded, security and the police were everywhere. It was the third time the school had been on total lockdown. Police loudly banged the lockers as they walked the halls with K-9 units.

Thankfully, the lockdown only lasted halfway through lunch. If I had to endure one more administrator saying, "Be patient," I might have snapped. The panicked thoughts of, *I have to get out*, quieted. Color slowly returned to my face as I drank my fill of deer blood, that's how you handle homo hematophagy.

I had no cousins, aunts, uncles to scare me straight or to advise me to speak out in support of me within of earshot of my parents. My mom never mentioned her father or her mother, and I didn't pry, but I still wanted to know about them. When mom wasn't home there were always leftovers, ice cream, and plenty of chores for me to finish before I exited the house at night.

Midnight

It was a good thing that Carlos' virtual existence was portable because tonight our basketball team was playing Lakewood High for the city title. My body was ready but the echoes still dominated my mind. I had to keep it together, just two and a half more months to go. I slowly walked around campus, shaken more by the voices than by the stabbing of a student right outside of my first period class.

The powder blue sky gave way to a distant scarlet sunset. With everything on my mind the walk to the girl's locker room was unusually long. I tried to remain reflective as I changed into my uniform. I could hear the crowd cheering and chanting trough the walls of the locker room. I sat in front of my locker and closed my eyes for a minute. I took a deep breath, got up, and entered the main gym.

Twenty girls stood on the basketball court stretching and warming up. The basketballs were on racks at the end of the gym. I jogged up and down the basketball court low fiving my teammates as we went through our pre-game warm ups. I must still be agitated because even with a double take, our smiling, white, angel mascot looked even more menacing than usual.

Coach huddled the team together and went over the game plan. Because I was a vampire I had more athletic ability than the other girls, but some of these girls were the best in the state. I was not the only girl in Angel Beach that was being recruited by traveling teams. The gym was filled with spectators; my mother was one of them. She hardly went out so close to home.

"Distribute, distribute, distribute... impact both ends of the floor," coach said over the loud music. "Active hands, secure the ball. Monica, draw in the defense, kick it out. Amber, push the ball. Trust the system and trust each other," he said. We were really fired up as we ran out on the court.

The game was very competitive and with one minute remaining, we were down by one point. The Lakewood girls were quick. They had been driving the lane and kicking the ball out for threes all night. Lakewood's three point shooters hugged the edges all game. This was not one of my better games. I played over my head the entire game. Monica led a late surge from us that caused Lakewood to call a timeout with thirty seconds remaining.

Lakewood put their starters back into the game. We were being outplayed, but Coach Ferg didn't panic. The crowd started foot stomping in the bleachers as chants of "Go Beach, Go Beach!" rose from the crowd. Coach didn't say a word; he just took that minute to stare each of us in the face.

During the timeout, I smelled him. I looked over my shoulder and there he was. The timeout was over. Lakewood inbounded the ball and slowly walked the ball up court as the clock quickly winded down. I saw their guard call out the play as she approached half court.

The Lakewood girls were older, bigger, and more experienced than I was, but they didn't know the difference between loving to win and hating to lose. It was the difference between Me Ball and We Ball, a difference the night air had just delivered to me. It was the first time I felt what could only be described as school spirit. I actually cared if we won the title. I cared if we won to the state championships in two weeks. I cared what he thought.

The rim was closer, and the ball moved slower. All of the players seemed to stand still. Time on the clock seemed to freeze as I knocked the ball loose. I outran her to the loose ball. From the corner of my eye, I saw the crack of a smile on coach's face as his clipboard floated to the floor.

The roar of the crowd followed me as I sprinted toward our basket, trailed by everyone. I swooped down the lane towards the rim and launched into the air. A collective sigh came from my teammates; the crowd hushed as I dunked the ball and briefly hung on the rim. The buzzer sounded and time expired. I glided back to the floor and the gym erupted.

My team surrounded me, shouting, people yelled, "She dunked!" and "Guardians, we did it!" Between the raised hands, I saw my mother's frown. She got up to leave, and as she did, she shook her head and "Amber, power doesn't show off... we need to talk," was projected into my head.

I grabbed my uniform with pride, looked at the crowd, and exclaimed, "Who brought the title back?"

"Angel Beach, Guardians! Angel Beach, Guardians!" was the chanted response. I panned over eyes, noses, and teeth until I found his face. Every day, my nipples greeted Adrian. It had always been imperceptible, until just now when I hugged him.

Adrian had a driver's permit, but he rolled a tricked-out electric blue scooter with white pinstripes. He said that he spent two years modifying it. It was lowered with black mesh, pegs, after market headlights, glowing blue running lights, and a modified dash or something like that.

The way he talked about the thing, you'd think it was his child. It was actually kind of cute, though. The scooter was fast enough to take your breath away, well mine, anyway, and it sounded more like a motorcycle than a scooter. It was sleek and, most importantly, it could handle two people.

I liked the scooter. After I changed clothes he wanted to walk me home, so I let him. As we walked, he reached over with his left hand and took my right hand into his own.

"We're both playing for city championships. You were really something tonight," he stated.

"Not so fast, my team won the title, you still have to."

"Right... right. But either way, I'm blessed."

He had a different tone and his eyes were glazed over as if he was in deep thought. I couldn't look at him when he was like that. My body had already revealed more than I would like and I was afraid my face would reveal even more. I looked away into the dark middle distance because now he's even more attractive.

"When we met, you said something about dunking, but girl you must have wings or something," he said. "You might be ready for a little one-on-one."

"Well, we'll see," was my response.

I really wasn't even trying to dunk. The night air was cold and I was gaining strength. Adrian and I had spent a lot of time together and every time I get the chance to really express myself, I lose the nerve. I quickly swung around toward him and opened my mouth, but no words were there. I looked in his direction as if to say, "I just want you to hold me," but again, I didn't.

The wind quickly whistled by and he brought me closer to him so he could put his arm around me. I felt secure.

"From the moment I met you, I knew you were different," he said, looking up at the night sky.

"Good different, or bad different?"

"Good different, definitely. Different like no other any girl I've ever met before."

"So, you feelin' a sista, huh?" I said in an understated way.

After a few moments, he broke the silence. "I am feeling you. You know that I'm a Christian."

"I know. I like that faith is the foundation of your life."

Midnight

"You came to church with me, but you never talk about religion or your beliefs," he said probing.

"I believe in an all-knowing, all-encompassing power. I believe that there is a Creator of all things and that Creator flows through each of us."

As much as I wanted to I couldn't just blurt out that I knew there was a higher power. And that the higher power created humans and vampires like me. I couldn't tell him that I knew God existed and that knowing gave even the cursed hope. That knowing was really the only hope the vampire had. I couldn't tell him that my coven descended from the first woman. I could not reveal that The Source of all life was far more powerful than Zeus or any Norse god humans had conjured up.

With so many things that could go wrong, with so many things that could end a life at anytime, a person had to be blessed to survive those elements. There had to be some force, something tying it all together, right. Vampires could not be born to die and not believe. Every vampire was born in blood and every vampire absolutely believed in God.

"Was it hard on you when your parents' separated?"

"That's what happens when you don't see eye to eye. The separation was probably harder on them than it was on me. What about your parents?" I said to change the subject.

"My dad and my mother have been married about twenty three years."

"Do you get along with them?"

"No matter what, my parents are focused on helping me to succeed in life. They want me to succeed as a student, as an athlete, and as a person." Adrian's voice has a masculine quality to it. His voice excited and calmed me. Through his voice, you could tell how strong his convictions were. I felt the positive vibrations when he spoke about his family.

"Your parents are doing a good job raising you," I offered.

"Sometimes, I think I'm trying too hard to please them," he said, seeming to reflect on his life.

"You are doing a lot of things, but you've got to be happy with yourself first," I added.

"Maybe, but something always seems to be missing." He looked pensive as another vehicle whizzed by. I wanted him to be forward, but he respected me too much for that.

"What's missing?"

"Love, maybe. I mean, I've seen love, but I've never been in it."

"Me either," I quickly said before I could stop myself. He smiled at my admission. It took us forty minutes to walk the three blocks to my house. A light mist and a thick nervousness surrounded us as we reached the front of my house.

"My father says the question isn't how many fifteen year olds have truly been in love. The question is how many adults even know what love is to show it?"

"One day, maybe we'll both find love," I said.

"One day," he said, clutching me as we gazed into each other's eyes.

I felt closer to him now more than ever. This can't all be just a coincidence. "Adrian," I said just above a whisper. "I was praying that we would have a moment, alone." Maybe there was, indeed, power in prayer. There was 'vampire power,' so there had to also be 'human power'. People of faith had a way of transforming objective reality into a palpable waking dream.

"Are you ready?"

"Definitely…"

Midnight

He held me close, our eyes met and the world stopped spinning. I felt like we were touching, I thought we are touching. A cold silence came over us as the fog swirled at our feet. For that moment, we held onto the fierce urgency of now. Maybe the hug after the game gave away too much, but right now I really don't care. I stood on my tiptoes. I opened my mouth slightly and closed my eyes as he leaned in to me. This was the best moment of my life.

As soon as our lips touched, the porch light turned on, hitting us both in the face.

"Amber, is that you?" said my mother from the front porch. *Damn!*

Mom says she's always in the right place at the right time. Her sayings are proving to be more and more… annoying. We gave each other a brief hug, but even the hug seemed to last half the night. In the hug, I could feel his heart crashing against his chest. Nothing had gone the way I had pictured it. It wasn't a kiss, but I still tingled.

Adrian and I finished saying our goodbyes and I turned to enter my house. I heard Lauren Hill playing and all I could think about was what my mom was going to say. Bringing a human home wasn't crazy, it was downright insane. I hurried through the door, hoping to avoid an angry confrontation. I quickly walked past my mother, who stood by the door with both her hands on her hips and a disapproving look on her face. I was rushing through the living room when I heard her voice behind me.

"Who was that boy you were hugging in front of our house?" she said as soon as the door closed. I was afraid of how she would react; she might forbid me to see him, so I took a moment to ponder just how to react to the question.

"Mom, that's Adrian. You remember Adrian... the one I told you about. And no, I didn't kiss him," I answered, hoping that my sharp reply would end the conversation.

"Don't play games with me," Mom said.

In my household and in our coven, we always tried to tell each other the truth. She could sense when I was lying, so there was no reason to continue. I may as well tell her the truth and deal with whatever her reaction may be. Well, that would be the mature way to handle the situation, I told myself.

"So this is same boy with the Valentine's flowers for you. The boy I've been hearing so much about?" she asserted. I nodded my head. "You've been a student here for four months, and you've already got a boyfriend?" she swiftly said.

"He's not my boyfriend. I hang out with other boys. He's in my Chemistry class. He's a good student and a good person." was my pre-emptive defense. "He's funny, too."

"He's always quiet around me."

"We are always laughing."

"You two seem pretty close. Does he know about you?" She asked the question I knew was coming.

"What do you mean by that?" I quizzed, trying to further gauge her mood.

"I said does this Adrian person know that we are vampires?" Mom asked directly.

"No." I decided to answer that question directly. "I haven't told him anything about my vampireness," I said, hoping that my sarcasm would end the conversation and ease my mother's concerns. So far, none of my fifteen year old tactics had worked on my mother.

Midnight

"Is he the reason you were showing off in the game tonight?" Mom asked, already knowing the answer.

I slowly nodded my head. Before she was worried about me fitting in at a new school, now she was worried about me starting a relationship. Well, I thought it was a relationship. After all, I was fifteen.

"Mom, he is smart," I began.

"So he's a good student?" Mom chimed in.

"Yes, ma'am, and he is a point guard on the boy's varsity basketball team."

"You've told me that before, I want to know about his family. Who are these Reznors?" Mom queried.

It was a question I did not anticipate and the smile left my face. "The Renzors are Christians. His father is an accountant and a minister at Second Baptist Church."

"Christians!" she exclaimed incredulously. "Baby girl, it sounds like this Adrian is a real nice kid. His family seems all well and good, but I saw you lose control in front of everyone. We can't have that, come sit by me."

"I know Mom. I got carried away," I said as I sat next to my mother on the couch. She styled my hair.

"He is a human and you're a vampire. You have to realize that most human beings will not accept our kind. I'm not saying that your friendship with him is wrong. You need to be careful. He should know better than trying to kiss anyone in front of their parent's house."

"Well, Mom, it wasn't exactly all on him."

"I know that you know better."

"You're right. I don't know what came over me."

"And, that's the problem. Does he know that you've been hanging on roofs top at night? Does he know that you run through parks before dawn?" My mom asked.

"No. How did you…"

"I am your mother, aren't I?"

"I spend hours wandering power plants, combing alleys, walking roof ledges, and sitting on fire escapes. The half-souled have to have something to do while their parents are off at book clubs, right?" I retorted.

My mother smiled. "Fair enough… fair enough. I just want you to doing something constructive with your time."

"What am I supposed to be doing?"

"I can't tell you that. Now, come here and give your mother a big hug." The hug she gave me was so welcoming. I was glad she didn't give me a long, drawn out speech about bees and birds

"I'm still having the vampire echoes." I brought up the subject directly.

"Still?" she asked as she walked into the kitchen to make us some hot chocolate. "What do they say?"

"Remember who I am… and stuff like that." I intentionally left out the part about Adrian.

"What else did the vampire echoes say?" she asked, knowing I was holding something back.

I decided to tell her everything. "Fine! The echoes warned me about trusting anyone, particularly humans," I blurted out.

"Amber, echoes are a way for our ancestors to communicate with us. They are ancestral guides that can help you find the way when you are lost. They can connect you when you're disconnected. It's like DNA, only louder. It seems likes these echoes are occurring because of the feelings you have for him." Her voice was stern on that.

That was exactly what I feared; she would blame Adrian for the echoes. I knew they would be an excuse for her to forbid me to see him, and here it comes…

Midnight

"These echoes are warnings, but they cannot tell you what's going to happen next because that's up to you. You are the one who has to live with your choices. These feelings you have for him may be real, they may be just a little girl crush. If they are real, you have to nurture them. Don't bottle them up inside of you. Relationships are tricky, sometimes, you have to grab a hold of them until they hold you back," she said.

"So you don't want me to stop seeing him?" I asked as she gave me my hot chocolate.

"Why would I do that? I think you can make your own decisions and accept any mistakes that may come along with those decisions. My only advice is that you be mindful because I don't want him to get hurt," she said seriously.

I once felt my dad in my mind, it was uncomfortable. Since I am vampire I can actually feel my mom inside my mind. She said that wading through the bad relationships and the random decisions inside the teenage mind was an unpleasant chore. She preferred that I communicate with her like this, on my own terms. Mom made me feel like I was a responsible, capable young lady.

"Mom, can vampires and human beings really love each other?"

My mom looked at me in silence for exactly three minutes and twenty four seconds before she spoke. "You know, that's a good question, which brings us to this week's lesson." I smiled at her. I began to enjoy the lessons in blood my mother provided.

"I know you and your girlfriends in between hallway make out sessions, study groups, and all day flirting, think about sex. I hear them talking about what you're going to do to this person or that person. I won't act like sex is a bad thing, but you girls seem to be in such a hurry.

"Sex is not a good place to start any relationship. Rushing into sex will only them into one of those ladies that believe love has never been kind to them. Most people never had love within them to ever be loved in the first place. There are many things to feel guilty about in life, loving someone shouldn't be one of them.

"A vampire can spend lifetimes searching for their mate. We bond with our mates and cannot bond with another, this bond is unbreakable. When we find our mate, it isn't just a physical pull. It is the true other half of yourself. If your mate is in pain, you will feel that pain. A mate can sense where the other is when they are apart.

"Having sex is one thing, making love is something else. For a vampire, making love is a near death experience, but it is an experience that sustains us. For the male vampires, just as it does in male humans, constantly having sex shortens your life.

"I see the girls at your school hugged up with a different person each week. I see dudes pop in and out of their lives like ducks at a shooting gallery. Every one of them worried to death about being off trend. How they feel on the inside is expressed by their outside actions and by wearing clothes that hide their personality. For a time, relationships are the best lies we tell each other.

"Every day going through life, thinking about how to behave so as not to scare people, how not to trigger their contempt is tough. Every single day having to think about how to dress, how to walk, how to talk, and how to respond to the police is hard work and it's harder than any job most adults have.

"So, I don't judge you girls because never before has there been a time when children are constantly inundated with so many images of sex, drugs, and violence, but if I did judge, by your conversations, I would think that your friends' lives are full of four letter words."

"Mom, some of my friends use three letter words," I remarked as I continued to blow my hot chocolate.

"So, now they are all your friends?" she sarcastically stated. "I realize that you live in a different time. A time when the names of superstar entertainers tumble out of the mouths of presidents, and First Ladies dance with grade school children. This is a time when war is fought by robots, and there is a pill for everything, including happiness.

"Hell, they are showing Grammys rap awards in prime time. It is not usual for suburban schools to be shot up. It's now comfortable to have a baby solo, and although we are long removed from the interracial days of shows like *I Love Lucy*, mixed faces frequently show up on screens big and small screens.

"But Amber, in the midst of this upheaval, the vampire obligations remain the same. Our goal is to survive. Many vampires did not survive the flood, wars, and the global enslavement of Africans. Thankfully, there were colonies of vampires living free and vampires mixed into indigenous tribes thousands of years before the arrival of European men.

"Many clans were lost in these human encounters; even more were lost during the middle passages. They were unable to feed daily and too weak to survive the long trip from Africa. We survived by imbedding ourselves into dominate cultures, others were born with the Lucifer Gene."

"The Lucifer Gene, what's that?"

"Vampirism is not an infection. Vampires can only be born, not made. There are beings that carry the vampire gene. These Lucifer genes wait for a more hospitable time for vampires. The Lucifer Gene is a dormant family trait that is part of a vampire's survival mechanism. In dire times, this gene was encoded into some of our children and they grew up as human. The like quality from a vampire bite turns on the vampire codes within them and they become one."

"So, there are other vampires out there that don't know that they are vampires?"

"Well, they aren't vampires... not yet."

"I wonder how many there are?" I mused out loud.

"Make no mistake, to not be blessed is to be cursed, but within that curse there are blessings. For those that become vampire, the process is a very painful one and depending on how long one has been only human, it can be very dangerous. These awakening vampires are covenless, elderless descendants of vampire tribes that may no longer exist."

"Have you ever seen one?"

"I have seen a few. I wasn't always a hairstylist you know. A newly transformed vampire awakens starved, dehydrated, disoriented; its judgment is clouded by competing impulses. Soon those impulses are drowned out by a fierce, intense desire for blood—The Thirst

"The Thirst helps us stay focused, but in those that become, they all set about satisfying it. Those that become have no center, no history, so they usually run afoul of a clan. A vampire council is convened and they are dealt with."

"Do they have vampire powers or are they like white vampires?"

"They have powers, some powers thought to be lost. In essence, an ancient vampire tribe has been resurrected with them."

"How do I know if someone has this gene inside of them?"

"You won't, even they don't know."

Midnight

"But Mom, you still didn't answer my question about humans and vampires being able to love each other."

"I was getting to that. First, you need to understand human and vampire lineage. Both vampires and human beings are creatures with souls. There are two kinds of man, the hue-man and the half-soul man. Adam and Lilith were created together; everything else is of a lower order. Much has been written about werewolves, fairies, and pixies, it is all fantasy. Even if those things did exist, they couldn't be communicated with. It would be like a human trying to talk to a bird or elk.

"Vampires are living, breathing, creative beings who are filled with passion, lust, emotion, and love. Vampires and human beings can love each other, but the relationship must be built upon trust and understanding. It is not something to take lightly."

"How does that work when your mate is human?"

"Amber you can never love a human mate as much as you need to trust them. You need to consider what will happen when he gets old and when he dies." She paused unhesitatingly. "... and Amber, he is cute and his blood smells glorious. I see why you like him," she concluded with a smile.

No way would father have had this talk with me and in that moment, I fully understood the decisions my mother and father made. They both used each of their strengths to guide me. I was thankful to have people in my life that truly listened to me. I hugged my mom, thanked her for her advice, and went into my room to change.

I left the house and headed for the nearest rooftop with thoughts of the basketball game, the upcoming state title, and how it felt when Adrian held me. Most of the time, he didn't see me coming, but he loved watching me leave. I saw him watching me.

I went from planting a seed to planting and cultivating entire gardens in my mind. I pretty much pulled everything out my girl toolbox and still nothing. I dropped from a branch and ran through a darkened park with thoughts of him touching my face and playing in my hair. Knowing what love is was not the same as feeling it.

Sex Ed. never taught me about love.

Chapter Twelve

After the city title game, I had a better grip on everything. Everything happened so fast that cameras and eyes only caught glimpses of The Dunk, but still there were stories about it. I no longer got that random, "Hey girl" from people who thought my name wasn't important enough for them to remember. I was known inside and outside of school. I participated in fundraisers and walk-a-thons, but none of it ever seemed to be enough.

When life shuffled the deck, sometimes the hand you're dealt had you living in the wrong zip-code. Success was due to hard work, but more often than not, in the Black community it was due to lucky breaks and arbitrary advantages. If the police did their job right, going to jail was your birthright and they'd be damned if you beat the odds. Even if you were a teenager, they'd pop a cap in you and hoped you had a prior record.

Some kids appeared to have, but they didn't have. Communities neglect children and some parents were absent in one way or another. They proudly claimed the title of parent, but set their children up for failure beyond giving them multi-syllable names. They didn't even think about things like that. Some kids were better off without their parents. A parent's decision could ruin the life of their children. Making that one delivery allowed you to pay your rent. Next thing you knew, you were making deliveries to take care of your family, now the authorities called you a crime boss.

If the kids managed to get to school, the teachers taught them like they had a better shot at grilling burgers and waiting tables than they had at running a business. Most of us looked for others like us to hold us down. Children could receive an education on the street, but the only course taught by the street was how to ruin yourself. All of these things occurred in close proximity to any school, any neighborhood, and any home.

At the same time, the guy you liked didn't recognize females by their face because he only dated girls with low self-esteem. You know, those guys that talked to you only long enough to figure out whether or not you'd give it up. Young boys gathered and loudly talked about what they knew or what thought they could do.

Every day, I waded through the, "I like your shoes," "I like your hair," and, "Good morning's." Most guys would say anything just to start a conversation with a girl. All of them wanted to be kingpins, but their case managers wouldn't let them. They would rather call you a bitch than by your name. Most of them can't even piss straight and they had the nerve to look in my direction.

They looked at me like they wanted to hit it first, as if I was just some regular chick. Even when you developed a connection with a guy, nine times out of ten they only wanted to get to know you well enough to have your first thong down around your ankles. That was the thing about me, my name is Amber and I didn't do anything I didn't want to do.

Worse than any kids were adults because they knew rebellion made it easy for children to be taken advantage of, which was how we are manipulated. The sexual innuendo

Midnight

that children were hit with on their way to and from anywhere was unending. Everything was sexual; music, advertisements, comments, but we smiled through it all. Adults figured we were all going to jump over the cliff anyway, so it didn't matter how many got shot on the way down.

I supposed that if I weren't a vampire I, like any other kid, wouldn't notice these things, but I was and I did. I saw everything that humans did. The way they walked. The way they talked. How they breathed. All over the city, humans answered questions with blows and anger. They went about each day harming each other with impunity. My visions continued flashing clearer and clearer images and the whispered voices grew louder. From Valentine's Day to Easter, I wondered what could be more undead than humans.

It was Saturday, the day of Adrian's city championship game. The afternoon before the game was the big end-of-the-year barbecue at Eldorado Park. Everyone who was anyone was going to be there. Touching a screen was easier than dealing with what came from actually being touched, but the weight on my chest had enough of hearing me say, 'we were just friends'. I was going to let him touch me. Today, I wanted him to touch me.

I had thought about this day a lot. His touch may leave me bare, but it was too late to be afraid of what I wanted. I spent a large portion of the morning cutting my hair short around the sides and back. I made sure the edges were tidy. I jaggedly blended the top of my hair for texture, which gave my face balance.

I was too into doing me to follow the personal life of some talking head on a screen. Perhaps I was too into myself, but if you didn't love yourself, who would? It took me some time, but I learned to love each one of my moles. Now when I looked in the mirror, I saw limitless possibilities. I finished my hair and walked into the kitchen. My place at the table was already set. I thought about how blessed I was as I ate my French toast. I smiled as I gulped down an ice cold glass of deer blood.

"Your hair is on point," my mom said.

"Thank you," I said with a smile. I finished my breakfast, hopped on the first bus I could, and headed to the park.

Eldorado Park was on the far end of Eastside Angel Beach and it was a massive four hundred green acres of paddle boating, basketball and tennis courts, bicycle and jogging paths. It had a glider field for remote controlled aircraft, a stocked lake for anyone who wanted to fish, and an archery range that was used during the Olympics. The park was one of my favorites to frequent during my nightly romps through the city.

As large as the park was, you could still hear kids yelling and blasting their music. The crush of teens that gathered downtown on Friday and Saturday nights had nothing on the number of kids in the park today. The group I was with was barbecuing in three different sections of the park. They threw Frisbees, played hacky sack, basketball and soccer, and those that weren't just tried to be cute.

I spent the early morning preparing two big bags of candied nuts. They were full of surprises from the cinnamon cayenne pepper on the almonds, to the sweet spice on the complex cashews. Of course, JD didn't believe that I actually made the nut mix, but everyone loved them.

"I'm impressed," Adrian said as he sat next to me holding a handful of nuts. The sun was going down, and we finally had a chance to sit next to each other. He had a sad look on his face.

Midnight

"Is something wrong?" I asked, lowering my shades to make sure eye contact was made. I wished my heart didn't leap, but it did. It was my moment, I was ready.

"I'm just thinking about the game tonight."

"You... worried?" I asked, standing up. "Come walk with me."

He slowly got up and walked with me through the park. We walked past the duck pond near the creek. "This is the biggest game of my life. Most of the players are worried about the television cameras and the scouts. I am worried about my dad."

"Your dad?"

"He doesn't usually come to my games, but he's coming to this one."

"You'll do fine."

"He's a hard man to please..."

"How hard are you to please? You know that kiss you didn't get?"

"Yeah."

"Did you still want it?"

"Of course."

He smiled and leaned over to kiss me. Suddenly, I ran through the park. "You'll have to catch me first! Slow poke," I said as he chased me. My laughter teased him as I darted between bushes. I ran over two hills before I began panting. I slowed down so Adrian could catch up. He caught up to me by a secluded clearing near the lake. He grabbed me and held me tightly.

"Damn girl, maybe you should have tried out for the track team," he said while trying to catch his breath.

"You're just out of shape."

He playfully pulled me down in the high grass. Underneath the warm hue of a yellowish-orange sunset, we clutched at each other and laughed like kindergartners. I propped myself up on one elbow, he wasn't smiling. Maybe it was the light wind blowing through my hair, or the subtle light that danced around us that caused my eyes to dance with anticipation. Once our eyes met I was unable to look away.

His brown skin, hazel eyes, and lips were to die for. I couldn't help but notice, as if for the first time, just how muscular his shoulders were and how plump his lips looked. My eyes slipped lower to the rest of his body. A body I had seen a hundred times in life and in fantasy, but a body which now seemed utterly different.

My lips brushed against his ear, and I thought, *Have my dreams come true or is the nightmare?*

Once the waning sun stopped peaking over the horizon, I could see once again. Feeling a surge of power, I ripped his shirt open. I shouldn't have noticed how his abs rippled all the way down to his jeans, but I did. "I didn't know you had these," I softly said as I ran my hand along his well-developed six-pack. He quickly caught my hand just before I got down to the top of his jeans.

He caressed the nape of my neck and with his left hand on the small of my back; he rolled over and eased my sleek body underneath him. He slowly dragged his fingers down my arms. His thumbs gently brush the outsides of my breasts as his hands traveled down to my narrow waist before reaching the curve of my hips.

I quickly inspected his face. The slightly elevated corners of his mouth seem to hold back his true feelings. Any closer and we would be breathing the same air. My breath stalled as his fingers slid between mine. His warm mouth slowly moved along my neck, causing me to squirm. He slid his hand up my leg; my heart was in my throat.

His hand held my leg that I had wrapped around his waist. His other hand slowly traced imaginary lines across my stomach. I could feel his soft lips on my shoulder. Through my tight, blue shorts, his fingers moved along the outline of my blue g-string. I let out a soft growl and slowly began grinding against him. His expression was intense, almost threatening. My heart raced. His heat rose, his veins called to me. I swallowed the hardest I ever had in my life.

I trembled, thinking that maybe he was angry, but before I could ponder it any further, he pulled me to him and covered my mouth with his. I responded immediately, surprising myself. His mouth was warm, his lips were softer than I had imagined. His taste was pure, sourly sweet. I bit and sucked on his bottom lip for a moment, pulled away, and arched my eyebrows before our lips connected again. He tasted of the sweet spice from the cashews.

My hands felt the muscles in his back trigger. Something within me has stirred, my pupils dilated as his tongue slowly probed my mouth. I grabbed his wrist, turned him over, and rolled on top of him. I had never seen his hazel eyes so wide. For us, time slowed as our kisses became more intense.

My low growls were the acknowledgement of a newly discovered a new level of achievement as I purposefully grinded along the raised stitch of his jeans. The softness of his skin made me melt as I ran my hands playfully over his chest hairs. My eyes rolled back as my blouse flew open. He tried to move, but the sun was descending and I was in full control.

His chest heaved as I fumbled around, trying to unbuckle his belt. The heat rose between us, causing me to press into him harder; neither of us were aware that we had floated off the grass. His belt was unbuckled; I devoured his mouth as if I had been starving. I quickly pushed away from him. I had been burned by his cross. I jumped up and paced back and forth, clutched my chest and shaking my head.

"Adrian," I said, trying to catch my breath. "This is all wrong."

"It's okay," he said, looking at the ground feeling embarrassed.

I was a second from jumping into the water from the sting of the burn, that's how bad it felt. I wasn't sure how to react to the burn or to his disappointment. I wasn't quite sure how to react to anything. I adjusted my blouse, shorts, and covered my burn. I looked around timidly. This was all new to me. How could I tell him that the kisses from his lips had awakened my desire—to feed...?

"Is it me?" he said.

"It's definitely not you."

"I thought we were... Tell me what's going on. Tell me how the way I feel makes any sense... you can tell me anything."

"I want to believe that. I need time and I need you to trust me. Do you trust me?"

"I trust you."

"I see all the girls around you... wanting... waiting... I want this to be real."

"It felt real to me."

"I don't want to be afraid."

"You don't have to be afraid."

"This is all wrong," I said again. "Come on, let's go find the others."

He took my hand and I avoided looking into his eyes.

As we made our way back to the barbecue area beyond the tall trees, I wondered if his heart was still beating as loud and as fast as mine was. Did he feel the slow burn that was now present inside of me?

"Where had you two been?" asked Jonathan smiling.

"Well, I've got to get ready for the game. I'll see you later," Adrian said, walking away.

"What's wrong with him?" Jonathan quizzed.

"Nothing," I said.

"What's wrong wit' you? Humph...something is wrong with somebody. You know those nuts were hella good... are there any more?"

This morning I woke up worried about whether or not I had any kissing skills. Now, I wondered if I could tell Adrian that his little wooden cross... I could imagine how that conversation would go.

Adrian, can you stop wearing your cross because I'm a vampire? Sure thing babe, can you stop being a vampire?

In between the salty sweetness taste and the burn from the cross was the thought of, *Hell yeah, I'm a good kisser.* I inhaled him. I tasted him. I have been feeling some type of way for awhile now. He had a girl putting love songs on her playlist. We weren't having sex, but his scent, his taste made it hard for me to keep things this way. I was not trying to prove a point in the park. I think we both felt something... didn't we?

I felt like a total ass an hour after leaving the park. The image of him was still unfolded in my mind. I didn't mean to rip his shirt.

Why did I do that? Oh, God! What if I forced myself on him? Did I hurt him?

MG Hardie

I couldn't trust myself around him. I think I dug my nails into him. Once I got back home and replenished myself, I pondered how unfair my haemosexuality was.

Our school was playing its archrival Wilson High. Angel Beach was located downtown, Wilson was an uptown school. Angel Beach was urban and Wilson was suburban. The two schools were as different as night and day.

I showered and made sure my hair stayed styled. I was so glad my mother taught me that funky, short; razor cuts emphasized facial features, especially the eyes. That's why I usually kept it short and layered so my curls popped. I slipped into a tight pair of green denim jeans and a tight, yellow printed shirt.

The night had fully draped the city. I rushed out of the house and within five minutes, I was in the school parking lot. There were hundreds of cars in the parking lot. The cars were not the usual school kids cars and there wasn't a beat up one in the bunch. It was just like being in back in Beverly Hills without the drug price mark-up

I walked through the main entrance of the school, crossed the quad, and headed toward the gym. As I neared, I could hear the cheers and stomps echoing off the buildings. Cheerleaders led the fans in a school spirit cheer. As I entered the gym, the crowd was cheering, "We are Wilson High! We are way up high! No one can deny! How great is Wilson High!"

I saw a thousand faces in the bleachers. On one side of the gym, people were dressed in green and gold colors. On the other side, fans were dressed in the deep maroon and yellow color of Wilson High School. Coaches were being interviewed by television crews. The game was so big. I heard reporters toss around phrases like, "He's articulate," and "He's well-spoken."

There were four times as many people in the stands than there were at my championship game the week before. That saddened me a little. I had never seen this many people from all walks of life under one roof. As I looked into the stands walking towards the Angel Beach side bleachers, I couldn't see how some of those kids made it through school when their whole life was a trashy, urban novel.

For example, there were guys flirting in here like there is no tomorrow. They were full of memorable wet dreams and crushes that they didn't know what to do with. They were everywhere winking, waving at, and approaching girls that wouldn't normally give them time of day.

Girls were just as confused as the boys. No one actually wanted a relationship; they wanted the show that a relationship provided. To some girls, young boys were the kind of puzzle they had solved a dozen times. Everything was cool until they found one they couldn't solve, that's how you get caught up. There was always someone that the best-looking people couldn't have and that ate away at them. They had character flaws so deep that no bleacher filled amount of preppy heels, strapless tops, and leopard heels could ever reach.

I couldn't tell what kind of character a person had, but I was observant. The beautiful had options and little consequence to their actions. Most of them spent large amounts of time covering up flaws instead of working on them. They were bad actors who believed their own press.

They had a dozen roles and the characters they played still hadn't shown any growth. They scored at the box office and had fans, so they never needed to develop anything other than what they started with half a dozen relationships ago. There was no life to their underwritten characters.

For those girls, their day was spent posing, pursing lips, swaying hips, attracting attention, and acting like they weren't doing it on purpose, but they are. Aside from designer clothes and countless hours in the mirror, the rest of their day was spent hacking people, this guy, that one.

The man of your dreams isn't much of a challenge for these girls. However, not all of them were successful in their attempts to be trifling. Most of them were just beautiful enough, sassy enough, and vulnerable enough to make you understand why some people followed them around like puppy dogs.

They never really developed people skills because why would you need those when you always get what you want? Speaking of being a Hateroni, take Leanina Jordan, for example. She was the leader of the popular girl's crew. The other members of that crew were Irene, loud ass Flatchestca… I mean Francesca, Monica, and a few other girls. They talked shit to everyone, but they really gave freshmen the business.

It is as if she always had an extra helping of dumbass with her breakfast. She constantly talked about how she was biracial. It's more like *lieracial* if you ask me. She brought her long legs around throwing shade, talking mess, swinging her hips, and tossing her hair about.

"Hello, Amber," she'd say and toss her hair.

"Oh, really?" Hair toss.

"Well, I gotta go." Another hair toss.

Besides her not know that leggings aren't pants showed that something was really wrong with her. Everyone saw the way she looked at Rick. Here she comes now…

"Hi Rick," she overstated.

Midnight

Every time she looked in Rick's direction, he nodded his head the way a person does when they were trying not to be disturbed from what they were really into. He really needed an "I ain't fuckin' witchu" glare.

She saw how deep and put together the brother was, and she wanted a taste. She saw how unavailable he was, how he was just trying to live his life, she desired the challenge. She wanted some of his Rickness.

Everyone's boyfriend liked her and she was every possible girlfriend's worst nightmare. She wasn't sorry about any of it. If you asked me, there weren't enough people keeping it real in the field. We all breathe a little easier when she was not around. Well, I knew that I did. There is nothing like being dated because you're in fashion. She knew the deal and here she is standing up to wave at Adrian when he jogged onto the court. Her hair is uneven and she's mad dusty.

"Here we go Guardians, here we go! Here we go Guardians, here we go!" A dozen cheerleaders dressed in green and gold, holding pom-poms ran out and performed a cheer routine. I felt like a normal high school student in the frenzied crowd. For me, just being out at night at the high school basketball game with all of the people was liberating.

Adrian had plenty of people around him who tested positive for haterism, but most of them were from opposing teams. They called him church boy and in a sing song Reggae way they would sing *Mr. Scooter Man* from the bleachers. He took it all in stride, especially if it was funny. He'd turned his head to the side and say, "Y'all the ones taking losses."

The gym was full of energy. The wooden bleachers vibrated from foot stomps and the game hadn't even started yet. I am surprised the old, wooden bleachers could support the weight of everyone. I scanned the gym for a place to sit...

"Amber, Amber, over here," Jonathan loudly called to me.

I look over and there he was sitting with our little crew. They were accessorized down to their socks, scrunchis, watches, all the way down to the finger rings. I was the only one not dressed in mostly black. My school spirit was showing. I even had two green and two gold ribbons on my blouse. It was great to see familiar faces.

"Glad to see you finally made it," Tiffany said with a laugh.

"Late again... the game's about to start," Carlos said while still looking down at his tablet.

"You realize that black early, is actually late," said Tiffany.

"There's your beau." Holly pointed. "Come sit by me. Girl, your hair is amazing, I want that," she said, motioning to my hair.

Holly had become quite good at twisting her locs, but even with all of her guided practice I didn't dance well enough to join the extreme double Dutch crew and I wasn't good enough to be her backup dancer. Tiffany did quite well in that role. Two weeks earlier, Holly sang her way to second place in the school talent show. She really should have won. I took my seat as the game started.

The ball was tipped and Wilson High got out to a fast start by making several three point baskets. Angel Beach missed shot after groaning shot. Adrian's dad was visibly upset. Coach threw his clipboard in disgust. Adrian talked to himself and teammates yelled for him to get his head in the game, still the deficit widened and the fouls piled up. At half-time, our cheerleaders performed and led the crowd in a cheer, but Angel Beach trailed Wilson by twenty points. Adrian had no rebounds and had missed all four of his shots.

Midnight

"We rock, tick tock, and don't stop! We rock, tick, tock, and don't stop!" smiling cheerleaders yelled as the second half began.

Halfway through the second half, Adrian was still pressing. The conflict inside compelled me to help him. Wearing shades indoors was something that I felt was incredibly pompous, but if I was going to help him, I had to hide the yellow glow of my irises. I put on my oversized shades and concentrated. The basketball, which was being dribbled by a Wilson High player, bounced of his leg and it was picked up by an Angel Beach player, who threw the ball to Adrian on the break for an easy layup.

Adrian appeared faster as he dribbled the basketball down the court. He shot a three and the net barely moved as the ball went through. The crowd erupted as he made steal after steal, and play after play. The Wilson defenders were powerless to defend against Adrian's onslaught. The crowd loved what it saw, an eight to nothing run and the pom-poms were up shaking.

"Who are we?" the cheerleaders screamed.

"We are A.B.H.!" the crowd responded. "Go, Adrian! Go, Adrian! Go, Adrian!" the crowd cheered.

"Guardians! Guardians!" the cheerleaders repeatedly yelled.

The crowd yelled its delight. A Wilson player fell to the court as Adrian took the ball between his legs and around his back. He darted down the middle of the lane and soared through the air for another layup. Wilson's coach called plays, substitutions, and then called a time-out, but nothing seemed to help. Adrian penetrated the lane and glided in for a monster jam. That made it a twenty five to nothing run. The spectacular dunk shook the rim and the crowd exploded to its feet.

"You got…" the pointing cheerleader said to the crowd. "You got…"

"Dunked on! Dunked on!" the crowd yelled at the opposing team.

Everyone cheered, everyone except for me, I was too busy concentrating. Rick playfully smirked at me. I don't know what to make of Rick, but at night, I still watch over him. Every now and then he'll look up to the rooftops to see if I am there, sometimes I am right behind him.

I was sharing power with Adrian, we were connected. Adrian felt invincible, even his dad was smiling. Adrian stripped the ball from a helpless opponent and heaved a shot from half court. The crowd was silent as the ball floated through the air towards the basket. The ball made a swish sound as it smoothly snapped the basketball net.

On the next inbound pass with five seconds remaining in what was now a lop-sided game, Adrian again stole the ball and went up for a vicious, two-handed slam dunk. Smash! The fiber glass backboard split as time expired. The game was over, the crowd erupted with joy, and Angel Beach High was city champs.

The gym celebrated as Adrian raised his hand with one finger high in the air while running the length of the court. The school fight song was background to the ear vibrating noise from the crowd. During the second half of the game, not one of his passes were stolen and he didn't miss a shot.

He looked for me in the crowd, but I was still sitting in the bleachers with my shades on. I was still transfixed on him. More fans rushed to the gym floor to celebrate the victory. He was surrounded by admirers. His teammates lifted him onto

Midnight

their shoulders and carried him off the court. He still held the broken rim in his hand, but he never took his eyes off of me.

My eyes had turned back to a light brown, and the connection was gone. Instinctively, I walked through the crowd toward Adrian. When neared me, he wrapped his arm around me. He gave me the smile of appreciation that one gives when your neck is lightly kissed.

"I knew you were different," was all he whispered into my ear before walking into the locker room. I walked away from the gym toward my house, wondering if he knew.

I haunted the city because the darkness brought about its own set of fear. I lost and found myself in the darkness. I prowled discarded sections of the city, always searching for something beyond trying to stay awake for fear of the occasional bad dream.

I ran away from the pep rallies, abbreviated conversations, the popular kids with expensive trinkets and easy smiles, the hyphenates, the techies and their popular misspellings, the people with stupid apostrophes' in their name, the rude kids who corrected grammar, and the posers who boldly proclaimed their feelings about the issues of others in hallway corners while sipping bacon flavored bottled water.

For vampires, the human sparkled when the sun was out and it was the vampires that radiated at night. Out here, at night, I don't have to wonder if my studies were a way of avoiding whether or not my sexuality was intact. When I was out there, the truth was as clear as night because even innocent girls liked to lay on boys for discovery.

"What kills humans only makes us stronger," was the notion drifting on the breeze. The echoes sure did leave an impression.

MG Hardie

"Adrian!" I shouted as loud as I could as I stood on the hilltop. I could still feel the after affects of the connection. I had done so much to get to that point in his eyes. I should've rightfully been his a long time ago. I made all the right choices. I made all the right moves. It would have been a wasted time if we didn't get closer.

Holly says my demeanor changes when I talked to him on the phone. Apparently, I had this lost look on my face and I addressed him as 'babe' and 'sweetie'. The more things that tried to drive us apart, the more we wanted to be together. On that hilltop, I relived the reality of it all. Tonight the city looked as moody as I was. This night was the darkest of the year.

The time would serve as the one to remind me of all the work, all the constant, practiced patience necessary to keep frustration from suffocating me. I realized the difference between options and no choice, a difference realized by separating pride from stubbornness. Differences I needed in order to grow. The difference it took to hold, and more importantly, to keep someone like him.

I had done more than ever to see that this day would be more than a goal, more than a replacement dream. I stood there on that hilltop filled with supreme satisfaction. I closed my eyes and recalled his scent. The burn was still felt but his kisses were an exclusive reward. The kisses were the difference from who I am and who I am becoming.

I could still feel his body pressed against mine. I put in the last piece into my jigsaw puzzle, and at the exact same time it marked the first day of many more days of discovery. I shouted his name again, but this time it was drawn out slowly as I tasted the sweetness of each letter on the tip of my tongue. He proved his love for me over and over until it became routine.

It was amazing how quickly you got used to the things you wished every day for, this would not be one of those times. There was no doubt that I had not made it easy. I was not his for the taking; he was mine for the keeping.

Chapter Thirteen

It was Monday and I was anxious to get to my first period class to see him. He was usually the last voice I heard before I went out at night, but he hadn't messaged, chatted, or returned any of my calls all weekend. I didn't know I would miss his voice on the end of the phone the way I did. My repeated calls to him were unsuccessful and I hadn't heard from him since the game. All weekend, I had a sickening feeling deep within my stomach.

I resisted the urge to go over there and stalk him the right way. After the city championship game, he said he knew that I was different. The scar from the cross burn sat uncomfortably on my chest, it hadn't healed. I knew Rick and Adrian were tight. That was his boy. He had questions after the games, so why wouldn't Rick tell him what happened in The Bottoms?

I told my mother about my first kiss, our first kiss. I thought she was going to tell my father, but she didn't. Instead, we went shopping. Shopping quelled my anxiety and silenced the regret echoing inside my head. My mom was full of surprises. There was no telling what my father would do; I hoped he didn't find out. At least, I could say that Adrian was Black.

Lately, I had been picking up more and more remnant flashes from my friends. I heard arguments, saw smiles, and I tasted blood. I saw my friends' experiences from previous nights; I could feel what they felt. If that wasn't disturbing enough, I no longer wake up screaming, covered in sweat. They are dreams and no longer nightmares; I am starting to enjoy them.

This morning I still moaned through five minutes of dry heaving. I had to rub my thighs for half an hour before they stopped trembling. I was doing all the things I shouldn't, fighting and lying. My mom was not particularly happy with me and on top of that, the dreams were intense as hell, damn it.

I entered the main gate of Angel Beach High and swiftly headed to Chemistry class. I arrived early and stood outside the door waiting. I was hit by a familiar smell, he was nearby. I wondered if my nervousness showed as he slowly approached carrying his small, black backpack. Before I could call out to him, he walked up to me. His smile changed as he looked deep into my eyes.

"We need to talk," he said, hesitating slightly.

"We need to talk about where you've been."

"I've been in fellowship, praying…"

"Oh," I said. The hairs on my neck stood at attention as fear of being the outcast crept back within me. Rick hadn't kept his word, simple as that. Never trust a human. I didn't know what I was going to do.

"I have been thinking these last few weeks about what happened since your championship game," he said.

"What happened is we both won and you played great."

"That's just it, I played too great. I didn't feel like myself, how did you make me do all of that?"

"What do you mean, I… made you…"

"You did some sort of spell to help our team, to help me. I saw you put on your glasses, I saw you staring at me the whole game, and in your game, you dunked the ball… I mean really." He spoke in a tone that suggested he was sure of himself.

Midnight

"What can I say, my adrenaline was pumping, but I can't do magic. You're not making any sense." I felt bad lying because dishonesty robbed a person of choice. I sure as hell was not going to just out myself.

"Awww, naw. I saw you."

"What exactly did you see?"

"I saw you wearing shades indoors and I know how you think that's rude. I saw your lips moving like you were chanting. You weren't even watching the game, you were just watching me," he asserted.

"Some rhythms never come clean," I said without thinking.

"What does that mean?"

"It means that some things are without explanation. You guys were down, you looked depressed, and so I was praying for your success. Thankfully, those prayers were answered, but magic spells... come on now," I said convincingly.

"I felt something, some kind of connection with you. What was it... voodoo?" he asked in an uncharacteristically deep voice, "It's dishonest!"

"Dishonest?"

"How can I look on these trophies or anything else I've done this year with pride... if I'm dating a witch?"

"I'm not a witch. I didn't even start attending this school until a few months ago and you were on the team before I arrived. Now, will you please drop this foolishness?" I insisted, hoping that would end the subject.

"How fast you ran in the park and the way you handled me in the park... there is something going on here," He concluded in a tone that let me know the subject was ending.

It is hard for me to lie to people I cared about, so I shook my head and looked submissive. I could see that he had an urge within him to grab me and make me reveal my every secret and had he done so I would have. As long as the words never came, he would have doubts, and he had doubts.

"Some rhythms never come clean," I whispered under my breath. The bell rang, thankfully.

It was time for class. We entered the classroom and took out seats at our little table. The other students soon filled the room. Mr. Taylor, wearing brown slacks and a blue Polo shirt, stood in front of the class and the lecture began.

"Students, today we are going to discuss the properties of Oxygen," Mr. Taylor began.

"Oxygen is represented by the symbol O; it is the element with atomic number eight. The molecules of living organisms contain oxygen. For example, fats, carbohydrates, and proteins contain oxygen. Major inorganic compounds also contain oxygen. Oxygen is the most important element on Earth. In fact, oxygen comprises most of the mass of living organisms..." Mr. Taylor continued to speak while he started a video that showed colored molecules colliding.

The lecture on oxygen was fascinating. I took copious notes. Adrian's face showed a curious expression. He shook his head and pulled out his notebook. He quickly scribbled something down, ripped the paper from his notebook, and passed it to me under the table. The note read, *You are my oxygen*.

I folded the note and placed it in my pocket. I smiled at him and he smiled back. My heart was settled as Mr. Taylor continued his lecture. I drifted into reflection last night's lesson with my mom. She knew a lot about vampire history. I didn't know that the Queen of Sheba and Queen Nefertiti were vampires. Each week, my mother grilled me on what I learned. It's two weeks before finals, mom was heavy on Roger & Zapp, but my nightly lessons continued...

Midnight

"The camera lens momentarily captures one's soul. Half-souled beings show up dimmer, pale. Vampires are not stable creatures; the blood we consume stabilizes us. All vampires drink blood but some don't just drink blood, some drain emotions, energy. Vampires are very conscious of authority and adhere slavishly to chains of command and lines of authority," I said as I stood in the living room nervously reporting to my mother:

"Amber, stop. You aren't giving a report in front of class. I need you to tell me what you have learned."

I took a deep breath and began speaking again. "Vampires don't just get energy from drinking blood; some vampires can get energy from strong life-forces. Some of us can even absorb energy from something like a lightning strike. And of course, there is always the trailer park vampire... not really."

"Stop playing around. What was last week's lesson?"

"That Humans and Vampire have a shared lineage, which is why we look similar."

"And what about the humans who think they are vampires?"

"The self-proclaimed, self-identified vampires... the wannabes." I snickered. "Vampirism is not something you can achieve. Maybe you can be transblack, but not transvampire. My vampireness is unknowable to humans. They have a blood fetish. Most of them have just watched too many movies. They've learned to enjoy the taste, but don't have a need for it. A person can't just say they're vampire, or have a surgery to become a vampire. Either you are vampire or you are not and vampire would never claim to be one. You can't be vampire by association. I actually find it flattering that a human would pretend to be one of us."

"I don't understanding what one goes through to becoming what they are is crucial. Now, continue…"

"All vampires have the need to feed. With puberty, we gain abilities… I am still waiting on mine. I'm continuing, no need to say anything. This need for blood grows when we reach puberty. We must learn self-control before puberty, otherwise, the thirst will rule over us and become Blood Lust. I almost forgot, no Allium Sativum… garlic."

"Right, garlic won't kill, but it can produce an incapacitating allergic reaction."

"Vampires can live for hundreds of years, so we naturally have a different view of mortality. Vampires aren't ageless, but you and dad don't look a day over thirty five." My mom briefly smiled at my attempt to flatter her. She's been thirty five for awhile.

"Silver is the only element we can't easily wield. Silver chains are like weights to us. It won't kill us unless we ingest large portions of it. The element silver is infused with the Lord's words,

"*The words of the LORD are pure words: as silver tried in a furnace of earth, purified seven times…*"

"…*Psalms* 12:6. I'm impressed."

"Silver symbolizes atonement, redemption, and God's promises to humans, I find that ironic."

"Ironic in what way?"

"It's ironic because humans betrayed His son for thirty pieces of silver, but God blessed silver."

"Hmmm… you are brighter than I was at your age."

"Rivers, streams, lakes, and large bodies of water are a no-no for us. We can cross over them, but not in them. Large bodies of water weaken us more than anything else. As for a stake through the heart, as if anyone could survive a stake through the heart... right. Umm, and we are overly sensitive to sunlight, but we don't burst into flames. And there is definitely no sleeping on native soil, my bedroom set is far too stylish for that.

"There has always been talk of vampires sleeping in coffins. I've never seen it, but even if vampires were to sleep in coffins, it was not like they'd be in dirt. To me, the term undead is offensive. Vampires are not dead. We are alive just like humans with slightly less obvious talents and sleeping habits. Oh, and we can feel each other if we are close enough."

"Very good," Mom said with a smile. "Is there anything you would like to go over?"

"Tell me more about Lilith."

"Okay, as you know, vampires and humans are brothers. Lilith was cursed, this curse is carried by her offspring, us. When Lilith discovered that Satan had seduced and given Eve a child, she set out to rekindle with Adam in the hopes of bearing his child."

"Did she go back?"

"She did. She offered herself to Adam, but because she had soiled herself with fallen angels, Adam no longer wanted her. Lilith returned to the caves, unwanted and unloved."

"Now, that's deep!"

"The child Lilith bore from her relationship with Satan cried incessantly, unsatisfied with the milk from her breast. She did what any mother would do. She allowed him to suckle, and suckle, and suckle until blood was drawn. After a few more sucks, the infant was quieted. Azazel, that first child satiated on blood, never cried again."

"Blood…"

"Azazel, a half human, was an outcast. Even among those sent to watch over humans, he stood apart. He had powers like no angel and abilities like no other human. There would be no blending in for Azazel, he was blood thirsty. He and other Watchers mated with, corrupted, and fed tirelessly on humans. Vampire and Nephilim armies rose up and spread. They overwhelmed human cities like swarms of hornets. These half-human children could not be reasoned with, so the great flood was used to wipe them out."

"Did it wipe them out?"

"Obviously not, we are here, but many were lost. Angel descendants are weak to water. That's why it was used to destroy them. Noach ben Lamech's family wasn't the only one to survive the deluge. The story of Noah's Ark was only part of the story. Noah was told to take in all the animals, the fowls of the air, the creatures that slither—all except the vampire. He was told to leave us behind!

"Before all the springs of the great deep burst forth, Azazel killed thousands of humans. He was unable to accept that he and his siblings were the only ones of their kind and that he was destined to be alone. He killed trying to unlock vampire genes. The great flood spared few… Azazel was not spared.

"Cain's birth brought a new chapter to the world. Cain, which means possessed, had the same father as vampire, but he wasn't a vampire, he was something else. Because of his villainy our *agnate* brother was cursed by God to be a changeling and was mistakenly killed by his grandson, who mistook him for a giant bear in the woods. Cain's wickedness has been passed down through many generations of humans.

"Akasha is said to have had the ability to fly. She was born in Uruk over 6,000 years ago she thought it prudent to kill her own kind to show her superiority. Grendel, the most noted of Cain's descendants, committed legendary acts of violence. Grendel is said to have possessed the Hellfire Ability. The dark side of man is every bit as vile as you've read. Many of Cain's most abominable descendants were hunted to extinction by other humans.

"Today, Cain's descendants are tame in comparison to Akasha and Grendel. His descendants have intermixed with descendants of Adam and Eve. They are indistinguishable, except that the seed Cain bore is the more sinister of man. They have no problem working with their vampire siblings."

"Wait... If Azazel and Cain has the same father, why do Cain's descendants have full souls?"

"Because Eve was blessed."

"Ahhhh, so Azazel was half-brother to Cain, and Cain was Abel's half-brother, but he was not the son of Adam."

"He was not, which is why he had no problem killing Abel, and that's all for tonight," she quickly concluded.

My mother grabbed her coat, "And, where are you going tonight?" I said.

"Out. Where are you going, young lady? And you better not say... out!"

"I don't rightly know."

"Well, be careful while you are sulking on rooftops."

As much as I didn't want mom's riveting lesson to end, it was over and I still didn't know how Lilith was killed. I only knew that first-mother had given birth to the vampire race and various strains of vampire around the world before she met her end. It was actually quite tragic to think of all the damage and pain cause by pride. Spending time learning with my mom always made me smile.

I snapped out my daydream to hear, "Oxygen is the third most abundant element in the universe, after helium and hydrogen," Mr. Taylor concluded his lecture. "Are there any questions? ... No... so that concludes the lecture."

"Thank God!" someone behind me uttered and class was dismissed on time. We slowly walked toward the door. I looked down the hall and noticed JD was headed in my direction.

"We are meeting up at the dance?" Adrian asked as we walked out of class.

"Definitely," I had almost forgotten the last school dance was next week.

"Great, we'll meet up at seven," he said assuredly and walked away.

I uttered a sigh of relief, confident that school was going great and my relationship was on track. As soon as Adrian walked away, JD walked up. He wore a light blue tuxedo with metallic silver stripes down the outer seam of his pant legs. As usual, he wore black eye shadow, black fingernails and no socks.

"Did I just hear you say that you going to the dance?"

"You know you did. Are you going?"

"Fa-sho, we all going. I hope they play some good music, something we can really move to. I have a new mating dance I want to try out," he said excitedly.

On the court, I formed bonds with strangers. The way the net snapped as the ball drifted through it always makes me smile. I stood on the court gripping the pebbled leather in my hands. The court knew me and all of my secrets. Adrian and I had both coasted through our regional games on the way to state titles.

Midnight

Our school hadn't won a title in three years. I was under much better control, mostly because those games were nationally televised. And we won state titles without me pulling a single trick though; I now held a school record for three point shots made. I was helped by the rumor of me dunking, so defenders backed off me.

Our football team lost in the championship game, so next year, with our cheer team and marching band beside us, we would show off our city and state titles in the Martin Luther King Jr. Day parade. I could already see myself while riding on top of the Angel Beach float, standing behind those proudly holding the city trophy in their hands. For now, the school year was ending and basketball season was over and the congratulations were dying down.

Halfway through the school year, the awkwardness had fallen away and now the school year was ending. There was very little to remind anyone of that scared, new transfer. *Everyone was addicted to something. Was I addicted to him?* It was the thought that filled my head as poorly trained dogs barked at me. You can always use a little sunlight on your back, but I felt the night Darkness was on everything I owned and it felt good.

It was the last Friday before the end of school and I hurried home. I quickly finished my chores and talked to my mom. After my chores, I got my skirts out and ironed them. I walked in to the bathroom, stripped naked, and stepped gently into the shower. Water ran down my well toned, supple breasts as I lathered with soap. I was starting to like my body. It was athletic, but still very feminine.

As the water rinsed the soap slowly down my legs, I felt overwhelmed by heat, a hot sensation in my chest. A sensation I had never felt before.

"Mom!" I stepped out of the shower and dried off. I wrapped myself in my thick, red robe and walked through the subtly illuminated living room towards my mother's room.

My mother's door swung open and she glided out with her right hand over her heart. "You feel it, too?" she stated.

"Yes," was all I managed to get out.

"It means our kindred are near, but this is different. A new vampire is in the area. Going to this dance may not be a good idea," she said.

I had felt the heat before in the past, but it was subtle, fleeting, as if someone was passing through or one of my mom's friends, but nothing like this. Mom must be going crazy telling me not to go to the dance; it was a huge social event that I had to go shopping for.

"Mom, I think you are over reacting a little. I promised Adrian that I would go to the dance and a promise is a promise," I responded as the burning sensation subsided.

"Ok, If you need me just call," Mom said as she gave me a hug and slowly walked back into her room.

It took me about an hour to get ready. I went through five wardrobe changes. After all, it was the last dance before the end of the school. I decided on black, ankle length, stretch denim to highlight my black, leather, gold trim, peep-toe stilettos topped off with a sexy, strapped, white print shirt with gold lettering. I accented the look with a light pink fade to gold nail polish that I did myself. I looked in the mirror, satisfied with my reflection. My mom thought I looked radiant.

Midnight

I said goodbye to her and she hit me with a touch of perfume as I left the house. I didn't really plan on dancing. School dances were just social occasions, events for kids to get out of the house. The truth is that dancing was the only thing I hadn't conquered. As I briskly walked to the dance, I was surprised to see the light-skinned girl they made fun of the day that I was agitated. I waved and she waved back. I was glad she made it to the end of the year… her name was Rebecca.

As I approached the gym, I saw well dressed people in a multitude of colors, a lot of newly shaved legs, well trimmed facial hair, and the sheen of hair gel. I saw my friends standing under a tree in the quad. "Sup, JD?" I asked. Surprisingly, he wore a colorful, sharply tailored suit and hard-bottomed dress shoes with no socks.

"Me, as always," he responded.

"Why didn't you guys go in?" I asked.

"We been here waiting for your ass and you're late as usual," Los said, snapping his fingers and rolling his eyes.

"Cut her some slack, y'all. She's here now. Let's go in," said Holly. She was in a mini beaded, black dress.

"Time to get our dance on," Tiffany added. She wore a form fitting, plunging, purple halter top. I saw her looking over my 'lance' cutout heels; she had on some cutouts as well, only hers were all black. "Something special is in the air tonight."

The heat in my chest lingered as we walked toward the gymnasium. I had only met older vampires and elders from other covens, never any vampire youth. I hoped the vampire was from a friendly coven. I saw Adrian's clique enter the gym with their short-sleeved cardigans and colorful assortment of casual tops, jeans, and sneakers. I looked for a cardigan with timeless horizontal stripes and slick leather sneakers, but I didn't see him. We entered and quickly moved to the dance floor. Surprising myself with how much rhythm I actually had.

Carlos was having a blast dancing with everyone, literally and some big booty girl has a hold of JD and I had and unbearable heat in my chest. Unable to contain the growing burning, I walked to the door of the dance. DJ Underage had everyone moving as I debated whether to leave or not. From behind me, I heard...

"If you gonna leave, to holla at yo' girl first." Out of the corner of my eye, I saw Tiffany on the dance floor with Rick, showing her Spanish Harlem roots. Next to her, Holly was two-stepping with Anthony, who wore a big Kool-Aid smile on her face. Now that's what's up.

The peace I felt was only momentary as the heat started to overwhelm me. I told my friends that I needed get some air. Outside the school dance, I was met with uncertain feelings. Suddenly, a remnant of ancestral memory called out to me.

"Cruelty and rage... Beware..." pounded within my head and the heat burned in my soul. The Lord, wounded by Lilith's constant treachery, destroyed our foremother. Some covens had not dealt with her destruction well and sought to enslave and feed on humans at every turn. Those covens made no bones about killing their own if they have to. I turned and walked quickly home.

The time was eleven p.m.

Chapter Fourteen

I was not one of them, all of them wanted to be alive. I saw them with their violet boy shorts and Vienna thongs. Not one was happy. They couldn't be happy, no matter how many floral pumps they owned. They squeezed their hips into open back panties and sauntered hallways looking down on everyone. They were on display with their sheer blouses that reveal polka-dot bralettes. The assault of butt buster Capri's continued as long as they batted their eyelashes at every boy and girl in school.

They want their brand new cheetah skin, motorcycle booties to scrape the vinyl floor to call attention to the tightness of their black, ruffle, and short booty booster panties. Their insides were cracked; on the outside they were on fleek as they pursed their lips every time they spoke. They were parasites doing anything they could to get everyone to look at their ass. They all screamed that they knew me. I didn't know any of those humans. I didn't want to know them.

My walk back home was the longest of my life. I was torn. I tried to focus on other things just to clear my mind. I thought of how I could name most flowers by looking at them, the weeds too. For some reason, I was able to recite all of Lesane Crooks' poetry and not just his; I could also recite the works of Richard Williams, Kimberly Jones, and Langston Hughes' just as readily. That ability most likely came from my nightly book feeding and music listening. Lyrically, I unofficially repp'd the west but it was the words, the music, and the rhythms of those that came before that provided me with inspiration.

Inspiration was what I needed right now…my mom, dad, the echoes, Adrian's suspicions, and now this other vampire. My mind burned with new feelings, new sensations. My mind burned with a new dream of me preying on humans, hating them, hurting them. I wondered if the damned and the blessed could love. As I walked, my mind flashed with all the great moments I had this year.

If I were to run into trouble with another coven, the elders would hear about it before my mom and dad. Crimes against vampire were dealt with severely. From what I had heard about the Light Festival, you had to compete against other vampire youth, which could be brutal. There were high of expectations and pageantry to the Festival, which brings me to Sarah Chang.

As I walked, I saw her. Her face slender, her body was petite, but sexy. Her jet-black hair hung down the middle of her back. She wore slouchy boots, a white ruffled tunic, and a tight red pantsuit accented by pink walking dead lipstick. As strobe lights flashed, she quietly strolled into the gym and sauntered into the middle of the crowded dance floor without speaking to anyone.

She moved as though she glided across the floor. She didn't acknowledge the existence of anyone. In the middle of the dance floor, she slowly bopped to the music. Suddenly, without warning, she reached out and grabbed one of the dancers; a tall, athletic, African American guy with close-shaved hair. She kissed him deeply on the lips. After kissing him, she slapped his face. He was surprised, but he liked it.

He held her by the waist and her red painted fingernails dug into his back, drawing blood. She licked her fingers and

Midnight

her eyes widened with a faint blue outline. The dancer wasn't caught up with the music; he was caught in her vampire allure. He was powerless to defend himself.

A techno-pop song blared as the students started dancing around her. In the dim room, no one noticed as she gently bit the shoulder of the dancing student. Blood welled up on her lips as she fed. Her fangs slightly penetrated the dancer's skin. The student tumbled to the floor and the flickering light covered her retreat into the crowd.

She had only a taste of blood, not enough to satisfy. A love song played on the speakers and the students were in slow dance mode. She walked toward the door of the gym. As she reached the door, she noticed Adrian Reznor entering. Adrian was now face to face with the vampiress.

"Hmmm… Grade A blood," she hissed. She walked up and put her hand on his shoulder. She paraded in a circle around him, grabbed his hand, and led him to the dance floor. She put her arms around him, placed his hand on her ass, and said, "Hey, superstar," as she grinded on him seductively.

Adrian turned away from her to walk out of the dance. She stood in the center of the gym floor and silently chanted. The music intensified and the students became transfixed on her as she gyrated her hips and thighs. She needed the attention, she wanted the attention. Everyone turned to face her, everyone except him. She followed him out of the dance and into the night.

I can't believe what I am seeing. I have to go back to the dance. This can't be real.

The images in my mind were clearer than the vision I had of the red eyed, thin lipped, bony Albino females who hissed at each other. In that vision the females danced around bonfires biting small animals and tossing them into the flames. This vision was different; this was something else; in my mind I saw this vampiress speeding away from the dance in her purple, two-seat sports car.

I arrived back at the dance just as the paramedics and police were leaving. Flashing red lights and blank stares were on the face of each student. The dance was over. Administrators urged everyone to calmly go home.

"What happened?" I asked.

"Some kid got hurt; he lost a lot of blood!" JD responded.

"Giiirrl, this bitch was all over Adrian," Holly said to me.

I knew the vision was real when Tiffany said, "You didn't see that bitch tryna steal your joy?"

It was those words that kept echoing in my mind. It was those words that prompted me to quickly turn around and disappeared into the night.

I leapt on the nearest building and was home in seconds. Once there, I forced opened the garage and hopped in the purple glow in the dark vinyl wrapped ghost white, clear roof Elmiraj, Mom's new caddy. I threw the car in reverse and barreled down Angel Beach Boulevard like hell had just released me. Believe me when I said that driving looks easier from the passenger seat, my emotional madness didn't help any.

I didn't know what was on the windshield display and console monitors, all I knew was drive, accelerate, and brake. The car issued warnings to me as I swerved in and out of lanes and ran red lights. The horn honks and screeching tires couldn't drown out the horrors playing out within my mind.

How mad could mom be? She didn't even drive the car. *Ready for the World* came out of the cars speakers the entire ten-mile drive, eight-minute drive to Adrian's house. I brought the car to a screeching halt in the middle of his street and I jumped out.

His scooter was lying in the street. The front wheel was still spinning; the key still in the ignition. Several red eyes cut through the darkness and darted toward me.

"Get her!" said a six foot, two hundred and forty pound Max Getty. He was captain of Santa Ana High School's soccer team and he was also the leader of the Albino clique. "Wait a minute. Sarah, you got us fucked up, her father is a legend," Max said, realizing what coven I was from.

He no longer wanted any part of this conflict. "Albinos, we are leaving!" he said and they glided over to their motorcycles and quickly left.

Sarah had a hold of Adrian as they stood on his lawn. He seemed to be under her influence as she moved her hands all over him. I ran over and pulled her off of the entranced Adrian. He tumbled into the grass and laid there face down, motionless. The slightly shorter Sarah slapped me and with a smile she quickly scampered up the nearest building. She jumped up various sections of the fire escape with the grace of a jungle cat.

I pursued her up the building. I chased her several blocks, over several buildings until she was cornered. We stood off from one another, meticulously eyeing each other.

"Who the hell are you?"

"I'm Sarah."

"Why him?"

"I smelled weakness all over him. I can't believe he's in love with someone a weak as you!"

"Weak... I'll show you weak!"

"I should have known it was the Uhura brood."

"Sammael, I presume."

"You presume correct," she said, smacking her lips. "Your clan is full of weak losers, they don't deserve respect. I don't care if your father is a legend. You should have seen your Adrian at the dance, he was all over me. He told me how you ran away because you couldn't handle him. I hate vampires who want to be human!"

"He could never love you. We don't kill humans."

"That's what the weak say."

"We are not weak."

"He is so good and so righteous. I'm going to have fun corrupting him. First, I am going to kill you and then I will feast on this human whenever I want. I can keep him mostly alive for years."

"It's amazing how the wrong girl seems to know all the right places to be."

"And... and! You said that to say what?"

"You're loud, trifling and this plan of yours is so not going to happen on my watch."

"Bitch, you don't have a choice."

"Is that so?"

"Are we not Vampire? It is the hunger that makes us what we are. Oh, you haven't had your first taste, your first taste of flesh yet? In your first taste, you can taste the salt mixed in with all the drugs, the alcohol, tobacco, all the years of bad living or you can taste strawberries, mangos, pineapples, and all the good stuff."

Midnight

Sarah's voice had an anxious breathiness to it. She had a pretty face; even her lips had no creases. As she spoke, I could see her hunger as her eyes outlined in blue.

"Human lover! Foremother was killed because of them. Because of them, your forefathers, my forefather, are still at war and here you are all up in their face hoping we can all get along. Trying to mate with humans weakens us and here you are cavorting around with these vessels! Pretending to be something you're not, protecting them over your own kind. Little girl, you disgust me!" she yelled.

Her eyes glowed blue as she launched a furious attack on me. We moved at speeds so high that humans would say they were artificial. Fist and high heels struck from every angle. I pressed my attack, but everything I did she blocked with effortless speed. Her right fist connected with my jaw, knocking me to the ground.

My attempts to get the better of her only showed my lack of experience. She jumped over a railing to deliver an elbow to my ribs. She was not Black, but it was apparent by her speed and strength that she had not spent her nights prowling buildings lost in thought or racing through parks away from her dreams. She had not just stumbled into vampire adolescence. She wasn't just faster, she was better. She had taken a different path, a darker one.

"Sarah, we've all fallen," I said as I stumbled to my feet.

"Fallen from grace to be surrounded by them... Little girl you have me confused with someone who cares..."

"You are really starting to piss me off."

"To humans, our very existence pisses them off. To them, we are nothing but an oversized, privileged bedbug," she said, rolling her eyes. "My coven does not walk in fear or willful ignorance of human kind. I, Sarah Chang, am proud vampire, bitch."

She was in desperate need of a hug. She landed a punch to my chest that sent me flying across the roof. I spun and landed face down on the roof with pieces of red bricks falling down around me. The cobalt of her eyes pierced the cold night steam that surrounded us. I slowly climbed back to my feet with craven irises. I tied my hair back tightly with a black ribbon.

"In another life, we could have been friends."

"How you figure?"

"You hate me because your boyfriend likes me."

"You must have the power to strengthen or weaken bonds..."

"Are you sure about that... little girl, you think shadow weaving is all there is to being vampire... there is so much more..."

Sarah turned, jumped, and glided to another building. I took off my earrings and followed her. It had just begun to drizzle as we jumped from building to building. We went right on hurting each other in spectacular fashion. I kicked her in the stomach; she punched me in the face. She grabbed my hair and pushed my face into a metal air vent. I flipped out of her grasp.

"I am going to do things to him you've only dreamed about doing." she whispered. "It's not personal, on second thought, yes it is!"

I spun around and threw a punch in her direction. She caught my hand and slapped me across the face, hard. It was one of those moments you never thought would happen to you, until it did.

Midnight

A whisper of "Stop" was carried on the strong elemental gust of wind that hit us. The wind staggered her and knocked me off balance. I would have fallen off the building if I hadn't fallen on my back. The hard fall on the roof put me in a daze. I had a lot of practice handling pain, but Sarah was inflicting new feelings of pain.

All I could think about was Adrian lying unconscious in front of his house in the rain and my eyes began to radiate yellow. My nails grew as the slowly expanding fog covered the ground beneath us. Sarah leaped a huge gap between buildings, raced to the opposite end, and scaled a taller building in one fluid motion.

I caught up to her and tripped her; she fell backwards onto the roof and thrashed about while I placed my knee on her throat. She threw me off and kicked me in the side. The kick sent me twisting through the air. I tried to run, but she yanked me back to her. We rolled around on top of each other, pulverizing vents and walls.

She freed herself from me, ran up a wall, and jumped at me. It was an attack I could now easily defend. My counter sent her body reeling into a large gray wheelbarrow that was full of concrete. Breathing heavily, she staggered across the roof and stared at me.

"I'm the alpha bitch!" I stated confidently.

"Boo hoo, a little vampire girl pretending to be human. Look at her wondering about human art, marveling at the poetry of the privileged humans. You're trying to be more human than the damn humans! You roam human spaces, you call them friends. Humans kill each other every day. If they had the chance, they would eradicate everything on the planet.

"Wherever we turned, we have been told where we could go and what we could do and how we could do it, where we could live, and we will be told who we could marry. With humans the perpetrator always gets caught, but it's the killer that remains at large, and still they love."

"I know."

"They are not safe in their homes, on the streets, at school, at church, and still they love."

"I know."

"Vampires pray on our feet with our eyes wide open, they pray on their knees with their eyes closed. We pray from a position of strength— we aren't called supernatural for nothing or have you forgotten?"

"Vampires don't have the luxury of forgetting."

"Then, you better recognize. Vampires are manifesting our own destiny. What you need to do is watch out... before I slap fire from you again."

I couldn't take anymore of her smugness and I swung my tightly balled up fist at her. She bent backward as I barely missed her face. She glided to another building with me closely following her. The building was smaller, darker; there was almost no ambient light. I cautiously stepped as I searched for her. As I rounded a corner, she speared me with her body. I lost my balance and fell off the side of the building.

It was one of those moments when everything was quiet, not even the wind was blowing. I could have used my mind to call out for my coven, but I didn't. As I fell, my mind descended to the first child trying to unlock his rare gene hematophagy, the repeated trips over uneven pavement, the heat of the sun, the breeze from the ocean, the new school, the friends, the snap of the net, the crowd, the underground rap scene, the Light Festival fire pillars, the boy who sparked my fire, the alcohol, the buildings I clung to, the church music, the foghorn, the shootings, the kisses, all the decisions that had been made, the choices, the nightmares... all echoed in the back of my mind. I am going to fail.

I looked at the heavens on my way to the hard sidewalk knowing that the only thing I really had was hope. Not that every day make you feel good hope, but a more of blues hope, a tragic hope. I saw why the attacks on humans were increasing, why the murders occurred. Why the depression within vampires had became rage.

Rage had built up from the things vampires could only talk about amongst themselves. In that moment I saw Sarah in myself. Life had no safety net. After falling six stories, I landed so hard on the sidewalk that the wind was knocked out of me.

My moans listed each bruise as tears were thick on my skin. I tried to compose myself and I needed to because she was quickly coming down the building after me. Crawling and gasping, thoughts of calling out to my mother entered my mind. The yellow of my eyes was nearly gone and I realized that I could not beat her.

"I don't know what he sees in you," she said, grabbing me by my neck. "I am everything you're not." With her eyes intensity glowing blue, she choked the life from me. Suddenly, Sarah let out a blood curdling scream. She felt an awful burning on her arms and between her shoulder blades. The searing pain of her flesh burning forced her to release me; she retreated to the nearest wall. In front of me stood a dripping wet Adrian with his wooden cross, the same cross that burned me with at the park.

"Get away from her!" he shouted.

"You..." Sarah hissed, clutching her arms and shoulders. Adrian continued to move toward her with the cross. She looked at me lying on the ground, and said, "Why settle for being human when you could be more?" She turned and leaped onto the next building. "The next time we meet, I break everything," she said before quietly disappearing into the night.

Adrian leaned down and picked me up. I was barely conscious, the yellow in my eyes but a distant flicker. "Hold on to me," gently fell from his lips. The pretense of knowing or not knowing was over, all doubts were gone. He carried me several blocks to his house. As he carried me, I saw vampire symbol variations on buildings where none where present before.

"I, I thought you were dead..." he said.

"Again, you underestimated me."

"Who were those bitch-made motherfuckers?"

"It doesn't matter, they're gone now."

"Amb, will I understand what's happening here?" I slowly shook my head no. "Who was that certified bitch," he said, slowly rubbing his neck. "... Another vampire, right?"

"So, you knew?" I said as he put me down on his lawn.

"I figured it out somewhere between the park, the game, and waking up face down in wet grass."

"So, you're not scared of me?"

"Not in the least."

I quickly moved to embrace him. My hands moved as if they knew I wanted to touch his smooth skin.

"Look at my clothes, the night, the dress, everything is ruined."

"Nothing on you could ever be ruined."

"We never got to have our dance."

"There is always now."

He gently held me as the mist began to rise. We swayed

back and forth to a music that was all our own. He looked at me in the moonlight with hope in his eyes and I looked at him with smoldering want in mine. It was our first dance. His large hand lightly pressed on my hip, which sent a shiver down my spine. I moved closer until my breasts was against his chest.

"Do you plan on using that cross against me?" I asked, pulling back from him.

"Not a chance," he said as he let the cross fall to the ground and pulled me to him. Then he kissed me.

Adrian must have cut his lip when he fell because I could taste his blood, it was intoxicating. My hands tightly locked onto him while I probed his mouth for more of the sweetness. My heartbeat sped up as his slowed. I could feel him desperately trying to free himself from my grasp. His struggles only made me hold him tighter. I suddenly released him. He slumped to the ground; blood trickled from his mouth. I slowly licked my lips, deeply exhaled and said, "I'm not a little girl anymore..."

The time is midnight.